THREE
Pennies

MELANIE CROWDER

atheneum

New York   London   Toronto   Sydney   New Delhi

ATHENEUM BOOKS FOR YOUNG READERS

An imprint of Simon & Schuster Children's Publishing Division

1230 Avenue of the Americas, New York, New York 10020

This book is a work of fiction. Any references to historical events,

real people, or real places are used fictitiously. Other names, characters,

places, and events are products of the author's imagination, and any resemblance

to actual events or places or persons, living or dead, is entirely coincidental.

Text copyright © 2017 by Melanie Crowder

Jacket illustration copyright © 2017 by Victo Ngai

ATHENEUM BOOKS FOR YOUNG READERS is a registered trademark of

Simon & Schuster, Inc. Atheneum logo is a trademark of Simon & Schuster, Inc.

For information about special discounts for bulk purchases, please contact Simon &

Schuster Special Sales at 1-866-506-1949 or business@simonandschuster.com.

The Simon & Schuster Speakers Bureau can bring authors to your live event.

For more information or to book an event, contact the Simon & Schuster

Speakers Bureau at 1-866-248-3049 or visit our website at www.simonspeakers.com.

Interior design by Tom Daly

Jacket design by Lauren Rille

The text for this book was set in Adobe Caslon Pro.

Manufactured in the United States of America

0317 FFG

First Edition

10 9 8 7 6 5 4 3 2 1

CIP data for this book is available from the Library of Congress.

ISBN 978-1-4814-7187-9

ISBN 978-1-4814-7189-3 (eBook)

For Dad

1

In the musty attic of an old Victorian home, a slight girl knelt beside a leaded glass window. Light seeped through the colored panes, and the trusses creaked as the house groaned, its weight shifting on the unsteady ground.

Summer in San Francisco is a foggy business, so while kids in other towns ran through sprinklers and flung themselves off rope swings into cool green lakes, on this twenty-third day of July, Marin stayed indoors.

Her knees pressed into floorboards milled in the previous century. She wore a striped cardigan over her bony shoulders and thick cotton socks up to her knees. A single crease between the girl's eyebrows betrayed the serious nature of her task that afternoon.

Marin asked a question aloud, her thin voice barely disrupting the air in the narrow attic. She tossed three pennies onto the floor and peered into the small book in her lap, the spine so thoroughly creased at that particular spot that the pages lay open without complaint. She scratched a mark on a scrap of paper and collected the pennies again.

Six times she threw the coins. Six times she made a mark.

The fog rolled in and hung about the scrollwork eaves of the house, pressing against the attic window as if it wished to see the *I Ching*'s answer for itself.

2

Owls are supposed to sleep during the day. Everybody says so. But an owl who lives in a big city sometimes gets confused about which light is the daytime kind of light and which is the night. And so it was that an owl who lived in the bend of a stovepipe between two high-rise buildings was awoken by blaring car horns and flashing headlights that marked the end of the workday. He blinked at the traffic shuttling below, and at the people scurrying up and down the sidewalks and in and out of cars, headed home for the evening.

OOOOoooo. He'd had a home once too.

Owl remembered when he was just an owlet, and the old man had found him at the base of the towering redwood tree out of which he had tumbled. His feathers twitched as he remembered the splint on his wing and the woven bamboo cage that held him until the wing was strong enough to test. Most of all, he remembered their daily study, and the pellets of wisdom the old man had shared with his little winged student.

Now that his teacher was gone, Owl wondered if he should leave the city for the quiet forests to the north. His wings wished to go, but his heart would not yet let him.

OOOOoooo, Owl thought. *OOOOoooo. The bird who chases two rabbits catches neither.*

3

Across town, in a beige cubicle within a large beige office building, Gilda Blackbourne stared at the stack of files on her faux wood desk. Her stockinged feet rested on the stained beige carpet between the tennis shoes she had walked to work in that morning and the discount heels she wedged her feet into whenever she left her desk.

Gilda curled her toes, stacked her feet one on top of the other, and sighed. She combed her fingers through her shock of frizzy red hair until the mass of curls forced her fingers to retreat.

It wasn't her fault that Sheila had had a nervous breakdown last Thursday and showered the contents of her desk drawer out the window and onto the sidewalk below. Or that Frederick had run off last autumn with the paper-clip heiress he met on an Internet dating website. But though it never was Gilda's fault when her coworkers left their posts, invariably their abandoned caseloads were added to hers. Believe me, there were many times when Gilda contemplated feeding her discount heels to the shredder and ditching the position herself.

Gilda did not like shifting children from foster home to foster home like chess pieces on a game board. She did not relish protracted legal disputes and endless court hearings. And she most decidedly did not enjoy being called to remove children from the scene of a domestic dispute. But there was one aspect of her chosen occupation that suited Gilda exceedingly well.

The arm of the government that oversees the welfare of children who are disconnected from their parents operates on a system of strictly enforced rules. And Gilda Blackbourne was a rule follower in the extreme.

4

Far below the city, below the dirt and the concrete and the cars, below the buried remains of burned-out row homes and carriage houses and cable cars, below even the bedrock itself, two massive shelves of rock slid past each other.

The sliding was slow, not the slipping past of cars on a freeway or ships through a drawbridge. It was the groaning, grinding sort of passing of two things that aren't meant to occupy the same space. Every so often, the sliding would jolt and scrape and the city above would tremble and crash in response. The crashing was a release of sorts, a welcome release after all that time pressing together.

But it wasn't time for that release, not yet. Almost. Soon.

5

In the city above, a woman stood before a tall window, wishing.

Her work was good, important work. Her home was full of friends and laughter whenever she wanted it so. Her heart was warm, her life was rich, and yet— Lucy wished for one thing more.

She cradled her mug of tea in both hands and blew across the amber water. The steam spread over the windowpane, clouding the rows of old Victorians and high-rise apartments dotted with yellow-lit windows and filled with busy families talking around dinner tables and bickering over things like television remotes or grocery lists or what board game to play that night.

Lucy didn't look over her shoulder and down the hallway to the closed door with the cut-crystal knob. Instead, she watched as the steam on the windowpane slowly receded around the edges and the city flared into focus.

She watched, and she wished.

6

Over the years, Marin had discovered several rules for survival in the foster care system:

1. Don't annoy, exasperate, irritate, or in any way bother your foster parents.

2. Don't fight with the other foster kids in the house. (Sticking to this rule was possible only if you avoided the other kids in the house, so that's what Marin did.)

3. Never, under any circumstances, tell anyone that you're waiting for your mother to come back for you.

If we rolled Marin's three rules into one, it would say: Be invisible. Now, you may think that makes for a lonely sort of life, and you wouldn't be wrong. Marin didn't have any friends, not really. She rarely stayed in one school long enough to make the kind of friend who sticks with you after you go.

She didn't have anyone who loved her. She didn't eat much. She barely spoke above a whisper. If she wanted something and she couldn't get it for herself, she went without.

But all that was in preparation, you see. When her mother came back for her, she would observe that her daughter hardly took up any space; she would realize that keeping Marin this time would be no trouble at all.

7

Memory has a way of shifting and dissolving and blending together. When Marin was four, she had hundreds of memories of her mother. They swam beneath her eyelids whenever she closed them: picnics in meadows and sleeping under the stars, circles of drums banging until the sun rose, and the two of them watching the waves roll in and crash against sandstone cliffs.

By the time Marin turned eleven, however, she had only three memories left. The first was of her mother leaning over the blanket where three-year-old Marin lay in a thatch of greenest grass. Her mother's face blocked out the sun, so that every stray hair glowed in a golden ring around her head. Marin's pudgy fingers reached up and grasped at the tips of her mother's dark hair, which hung in curling locks that swung toward the ground.

The second memory was a scolding, from a day when Marin had slipped a nickel through the slot in their piggy bank.

"Why would you want to save something as worthless as money?" Marin's mother shook the piggy bank. The single coin clattered around inside and Marin's mother let loose an exasperated sigh. "This bank is for wishes. Nothing else."

The third memory was of the day Marin's mother left. Marin would have traded that memory for any of the others that had slipped away from her over the years. But that one stayed there in her mind like a skinned knee that you keep bumping into bedposts and banging onto the sidewalk so it never goes away.

8

Gilda eyed the perilously leaning stack of case files on the corner of her desk and reached for the topmost one. She opened the manila cover and skimmed for pertinent details.

Name: Greene, Marin

Age: 11

Age at first placement: 4

Reason for placement: abandonment

Other family: none

Previous placements: three foster homes and two
    group homes

Comments: termination of parental rights imminent

Eleven is a tricky age in the foster system. Families are eager to adopt an infant with chubby cheeks and pudgy legs and those blinky eyes that haven't seen too much hardship yet. But when a kid turns ten or eleven or twelve, that's when the sad begins to pull at her eyes, when the *I'm not so sure I can trust you* scowl starts to carve lines around her mouth.

Gilda sighed and lifted a stack of papers held together with a paper clip. She peeled back a hot-pink sticky note that read: POTENTIAL FOSTER-ADOPT CANDIDATES. One by one she turned over the pages, jotting notes in the margins as she read.

The first option was a middle-aged couple whose own children were grown and who had discovered they didn't like their empty nest as much as they thought they might.

The second was a family of six who wanted just one more to make it a lucky seven.

And the third was a single woman—a medical doctor, clinical but with a kind disposition. Sheila had scribbled a star beside the woman's photo.

Well. We'll see about that.

Gilda shuffled the stack of papers back together until the edges lined up just so, and then she placed the paper clip exactly into the paper-clip-shaped indents. She closed the file and tucked it under her arm. She gave her toes one last wide-reaching wiggle and wedged them into her heels.

Proper procedure would be followed. Gilda was going to have to meet this child herself.

9

The cost of living in San Francisco is high—skyscraper high. Some people manage by working all-hours jobs. Others rent narrow apartments in old buildings and share with a half dozen friends. Another, less conventional way to make rent is to take in foster kids. Each one comes with an allowance from the state, so it can be a job—sort of.

But if you're one of the kids living in a home like that, where you're more of a paycheck than a person, you get to wishing you lived anywhere else. Marin had been in enough foster homes to realize that, bad as this one was, there probably wasn't any better one out there for her. If she ever moved again, it would be because her mother came back for her at last. She told herself that all the years of wishing and all the wants she'd swallowed down, hard as a horse pill and bitter as a spoonful of cough syrup, would be worth it when they were together again.

Marin stared at her reflection in the cloudy bathroom mirror while she guided her toothbrush in small jerky circles. Marin had always tried not to think about why her mother left, or worse—why she never returned. But something about being a walking, talking paycheck in this house brought all those questions right up to the surface like a splinter just deep enough that you can't get it out.

Marin spit, swished a little water around in her mouth, spit again, and walked with whispering footsteps down the hall to the room she shared with three other girls. The door was open, and as she made her way inside she saw all three girls huddled over something in their hands. It was a book, a small, soft-at-the-edges book. It was *her* book.

Sometimes being invisible does you no good at all.

"Give that back!" Marin cried, and she lunged for her book. But Ashley was ready. She lifted the *I Ching* over her head, where even if the smaller girl took a running leap, she still couldn't reach it.

"What do you want with that old thing, anyway?" That was Becky.

"Musta been her mama's," said Amber, the *ssss* sounds whistling through the gap between her two front teeth.

Marin grabbed Ashley's arm and tried to yank it down, but the older girl just laughed and handed the *I Ching* to Becky, who lifted it even higher over her head.

"I bet you can't even read it." Becky opened the book high in the air and squinted at the tiny print. "'Preponderance of the—'What the heck is a 'preponderance'?" She snapped the book shut.

"I bet she thinks she'll find her mama in there somewhere." Amber again.

Ashley clamped a hand onto her hip. "Her mama's nobody-knows-where. That's what happens when you get left and no one ever comes back for you."

"I heard them talking about it on the phone." By "them," Becky meant the adults in the house. "Her mama doesn't want her, not ever."

Marin stepped on the rail of the lower bunk so she was nose to nose with Becky. "You're a liar!" Marin kicked her in the shin, right in the boniest part, grabbed her book while the older girl doubled over, howling, and ran for it.

10

One might wonder, how could a mother leave a perfectly charming, rosy-cheeked, pigtailed four-year-old? It's a good question. But you see, not every woman who bears a child is up to the task of mothering.

Unfortunately for Marin, hers was one of those.

She had left three things behind: her pigtailed daughter, her pocket-size copy of the *I Ching*, and a ceramic piggy bank. As the years stretched on and Marin was moved from foster home to foster home, the little book and the piggy bank went with her inside a banged-up suitcase that also held pajamas, a few changes of clothes, and, if she was lucky, a toothbrush.

The piggy bank was handmade, with gloppy glazes

that had dripped and pooled and hardened in sharp nubs along the base. There was no cork or plastic plug to pull out of its ceramic underbelly so you could check on the contents; once something was inside, it was in there for good. If ever Marin held the piggy bank between her hands and shook it, she would hear a muffled rustling and the lone nickel still clanking around inside.

The little book was a translation of an ancient Chinese text called the *I Ching*. For millennia, scholars have studied the wisdom it offers, and people in every corner of the globe search for answers to life's questions within its pages.

When all you have from your mother are a piggy bank and a book, you don't let go of those things. When you need a companion for your lonely-day imaginings, the stout ceramic pig becomes your friend. When you learn to read, your mother's book is the one you choose. So while other kids were reading about a cat and a hat and a fish in a dish, Marin sounded out syllables to words she didn't yet know the meaning of. *Un-it-y. B-b-b-en-ef-it. Dan-ge-rrrr.*

Maybe the *I Ching* wasn't actually ever anything special to Marin's mother. Maybe it ended up by accident in the battered suitcase dropped off with the girl at Child Protective Services. Or maybe not. There were so many of those kinds of *why* questions and *how* questions that somewhere along the line, Marin had stopped asking some of them. And whether the answers she arrived at were the right ones or not, they became the true ones in Marin's mind.

Years ago, Marin had decided that since the little book had belonged to her mother, it must be the way back to her too.

11

The *I Ching* has an answer for every question a person may wish to ask of it. In fact, it has 4,096 different answers to offer.

But it never does give a person a simple yes or no. If Marin asked, *What will be the outcome if I run away from this stupid foster home with the nosiest foster sisters on the planet*, the *I Ching* might say: *Patience*. Or if she asked, *What will be the outcome if I sneak into the Child Protective Services offices and look up everything they have on my mother*, the *I Ching* might say: *Retreat*.

Today was no different. *Conflict* was the answer the *I Ching* gave when Marin cast her three pennies on the attic floorboards. What was that supposed to mean? Conflict like an argument? Or trouble with the police? Or just the everyday-life kind of conflict? The *I Ching* was anything but specific.

As Marin descended the rungs of the ladder that led out of the attic and then the creaky stairs going down two more flights to the sitting room, she barely looked where her feet fell, lost in the puzzle of her little book's latest message.

She was so lost in thought, in fact, that she failed to notice the woman in the beige blazer and knee-length skirt perched on her foster mother's sofa. A manila file rested on the woman's thighs, stuffed with so many papers that it was rounded at the fold and bowed at the edges.

When she finally did look up, Marin stopped with one foot dangling over the final step. Her fingers curled over the banister.

She knew that folder. She would recognize it any-where.

Conflict. Aha. Marin closed the *I Ching* and tucked it into the back pocket of her jean skirt. She dropped her foot onto the last stair and crossed the hall into the sitting room. Her feet met the floor so softly, they barely made a sound. She had so thoroughly perfected the art of going through the world unnoticed that it was only when she sat in a wingback chair opposite the harried social worker that the woman looked up from the smudge she had been scrubbing off her left shoe and blinked.

"Well," she said. "You must be Marin."

"I am. And you are not Sheila."

"Ah, yes, sorry about that. Sheila is no longer with the agency. I am your social worker now." She leaned over the scuffed coffee table and extended her hand. "Gilda Blackbourne. Pleased to meet you."

The two of them shook hands and then sat back, each considering the other. The yelps and bangs of the seven other children in the home hammered against the floors above and shook the dust from the sixties-chic light fixture onto Gilda's enthusiastic head of hair.

"A full house, I see," she said as her eyebrows climbed toward the ceiling.

"Yes. Very."

"Not the sort of place a person would want to stay *too* long."

Marin frowned.

"Let's see if we can do something about that." Gilda set the case file down on the coffee table and leaned toward the hallway. "Where is that woman?" Gilda craned her neck and tapped her toe as if she could summon Marin's foster mother with nothing more than her powers of sheer exasperation.

Gilda turned her attention back to the child in

front of her. "Marin, your next placement may be quite a bit more permanent. The termination papers will be delivered any day, and after the proper forms are filed and court approval is granted—"

"Termination papers?"

"Oh, forgive me, did Sheila not tell you? Your birth mother has agreed to relinquish any and all parental rights. You will finally be free to be adopted."

Marin blinked. Adopted? But that was for other kids who didn't already have a mother, kids who wanted to start new families. She slipped a hand into the pocket of her cardigan, which was weighed down by her small stack of pennies.

"You spoke to my mother—Summer Greene?" Her fingers gripped the pennies so tightly, the edges of the coins bit into her palm.

"How did you find her? You're sure it was her? And that's what she said. She doesn't—"Marin's voice broke and she clamped her lips shut, swallowed, and tried again. "She doesn't want to be my mother anymore? At all?" The light fixture overhead creaked loud as a falling crane. The still air in the sitting room pressed against Marin's eardrums like gale-force winds.

"Well, I haven't spoken with the woman personally." Gilda opened the file and began flipping through the clumps of stapled and paper-clipped papers. "The judge presiding over your case ordered that every possible avenue be pursued to locate Ms. Greene prior to a court-ordered termination.

"She was discovered and presented with the options of either reunification or relinquishment of parental rights so that you might be adopted. She chose the latter and signed all necessary documents per California state regulations."

Marin took in her breaths as if she were swallowing them, one great gulp at a time. Heat crawled up her neck like a rash spreading out of control, and Marin scratched at it desperately.

Her mother didn't want her? Not ever? But Marin hadn't even had a chance to convince her yet. It couldn't be too late already.

No. She hadn't given up all those years ago when every single letter she'd sent to her mother, unaddressed and pleading for the goodwill of the postmaster, had been returned. She hadn't given up when the kids in her group homes had, one by one, been reunited with their families. She hadn't given up with each birthday that passed, as she grew one year older, one year further from the memory of the two of them together.

She hadn't given up. So her mother couldn't either. Marin knew what to do. She had her mother's book. Just a few minutes ago the *I Ching* had said—

Oh, *conflict*. She could do *conflict*. Like the clicking gears of the plastic clock on the wall, a plan slid into place in Marin's mind. She tilted her head to the side. "Wouldn't you need to speak to the foster parents here to get approval for me to leave?"

"Yes, in fact, that woman said she would be right in to join us. Some people are incapable of making an appointment and keeping it. . . ." Gilda's voice trailed off as she tramped through the sitting room toward the back of the house.

Marin waited until the *clomp clomp clomp* of the social worker's heels rounded the corner at the end of the hallway. She twisted in her seat and peeked over the carved top of the wingback chair and then crept around the coffee table. She stared at the open file in front of her. There was her name (last name first and first name last), and a photo taken when she had entered the system at four years old. Her own face stared back at her against a stark white background. There was so much room on either side of her, she didn't even fill up half of the frame. The girl in the picture looked frail, and more than a little afraid.

Well, Marin wasn't afraid now. She was angry. Why did all these adults—foster parents and judges and even the most well-meaning social workers—why did they get to decide Marin's life for her? What about what *she* wanted?

Marin flipped through the clumps of paper as fast as she could. But she was nervous, so her fingers fumbled with the stuck-together pages. If Gilda was in contact with her mother, then there had to be an address somewhere. Or a phone number. *Something.* She flipped and flipped, her breath coming in short, panicked bursts. The voices at the back of the house and the indelicate clomping of Gilda's heels drew closer.

Any minute they were going to round that corner and see her. With a groan, Marin stacked the papers together again and shut the file. But the edges were sticking out all over the place—not at all like the neat package the social worker had left. Marin could hear the adults clearly now, just on the other side of the sitting room wall.

"But I need the stipend for eight children to make rent. If she's leaving, I'll need another kid in here by the end of the week."

Gilda's banging heels paused and scraped against the floor as if she were turning back to confront the woman. "Child Protective Services is not in the business . . ."

Marin tapped the edges, trying to straighten the

wayward pages, her heart hammering in her chest.

"...of providing you with an income ..."

Marin closed the file and scurried back to her chair. Gilda was going to know the second she came back in here that Marin had been snooping. And she hadn't even gotten what she was looking for. She'd failed. She was never going to find her mother.

"... so that you can maintain the life you are accustomed to...."

Maybe she should just grab the file and make a run for it. What could they do to her? Make her stay here? Stick her in a group home? Anything would be better than being adopted by some stranger when she was supposed to be with her mother.

"... This system exists solely for the safety and protection ..."

A gust of wind blew open the front door and swirled every which way—down the hall, up the stairs, around the corner into the sitting room. It ran along the pale skin of Marin's neck between the collar of her cardigan and her hairline. It ruffled the brown-tipped leaves of an ailing ficus in the corner.

"... of the children in its care. Now, if you will excuse me ..."

The wind yanked open Marin's case file and sent its contents spiraling around the room in a dervish of papers freed of their binds and gleefully cast out of order.

"Ms. Blackbourne!" Marin called.

The social worker stepped into the sitting room, her hair jettisoning upward and to the right like a hot-air balloon yanked off course. "Shut the door!" Marin's foster mother ran to obey.

Marin knelt in the mess of court documents and transcript pages. "Oh, let me help you with these." An earnest smile tugged at her lips as she stacked the papers one on top of the other. Let them think she was slow. Let them think she cared about lining up the edges perfectly.

Marin had been given another chance. She was not going to waste it.

Had Gilda been more in possession of her wits, it might have occurred to her how inappropriate it was for a young person to put in order papers of such a sensitive nature. But Gilda, having just witnessed her carefully ordered world thrown to the winds, was not thinking clearly.

So while the social worker lunged after wayward documents, Marin was free, under cover of the coffee table, to quickly scan the contents of each paper she put her hands on. She had no interest in the pages that detailed each of her previous foster homes. Those that assessed her physical and emotional health were of no use to her either.

She shot a quick glance over her shoulder. She was running out of time. Marin flipped through the last few pages—and there, at last, was a phone number. It wasn't the one she was looking for, but it would have to do.

The page read:

Date of surrender: June 7, 2010

Name of child: Marin Greene

Name of contact: Talula Walter, (415) 555-0136

Relationship to child: friend of mother

Reason for surrender: abandonment by last known relative

Marin folded the paper and tucked it into the pocket of her cardigan. She crawled out from under the coffee table and handed the rest to her social worker, who was still muttering about the selection process that allowed individuals such as *that woman* to be entrusted with the guardianship of children.

Marin helped Gilda up and out the door. If she hadn't been in such a state, the social worker might have been tempted to turn back around, look down her freckled nose, grip the slight girl's shoulder, and say, *I will get you out of here, Marin Greene. I will find you a real home, and a worthy mother. I swear it.*

But even if she had wanted to say such a thing, she never could have. In her line of work, Gilda Blackbourne knew better than to make those sorts of promises.

12

Talula Walter. Marin knew that name. At least, she knew the first name. It had always been there, tucked safely in the darkest corner of her mind along with the third memory Marin had of her mother. The one that wouldn't go away.

She remembered the whole thing, every single detail. She had been lying on the floor stacking a bunch of film canisters like nursery-school blocks on a small braided rug. Her mother was pacing across a narrow room with scuffed wood floors and a batik tapestry hung like a curtain over the window, which turned the sunlight into an orange and maroon and green abstract painting on the opposite wall.

"Summer," the woman with the long golden braids

said, "you can't just take off like that for days at a time. You're her mother. She needs you."

"The kid is fine!" Summer had insisted, jabbing at the air in Marin's direction. "Look at her. What more could she want?"

"A mother. She wants a mother who's actually around to take care of her."

"Get off my case, Talula! I'm telling you, I can't—"

"You have to! It's not just about you anymore. You have a daughter now."

"What do you know? You think it's so easy?" Summer planted her hands on the mantel, fingers spread wide. She dropped her head, puffed up her cheeks, and breathed all the air out of her lungs in a rush. "Fine," she said, and she spun to face them both. "You take care of her, then. I'm sure you'll do a better job than me."

With that, Summer left, her filmy skirt trailing behind her long strides. The screen door slammed, catching the tip of the thin cotton skirt in the door-jamb for a second before it slipped through.

Talula had run after Summer, calling after her, begging her to come back. But it was no good. Marin's mother was gone.

13

There were many reasons why Owl should leave the city.

No one here would miss him. And perhaps the forest would be kinder to his sore wing. He wouldn't have to fly so far to find food. He could rest in the hollowed-out burl of a towering redwood tree and let the misty canopy hide him from view.

OOOOoooo, Owl thought. *OOOOoooo*.

Really, there was no good reason for him to stay.

14

Back in her office, Gilda made three phone calls. First to the empty nesters. A lovely couple. But did she detect a wheeze in the gentleman's breath? And something of a nervous disposition in the lady? Maybe not, then, the right fit for an eleven-year-old.

So she called the family of six. But her questions kept being interrupted by banged elbows or pilfered toys and the accompanying yowls on the other end of the line. Gilda pinched the skin between her eyes and blinked several times. She rolled her toes in the carpet. A little girl could get lost in the rough-and-tumble of a house like that.

And so, she dialed the doctor. The woman had crisp, concise answers to Gilda's queries. There was no wheeze or other detectable frailty, and no ready distractions. There were, however, an array of available dates on which she could accommodate a home visit.

Gilda made the appointment and set the telephone down. Sheila had starred the doctor's profile before she left; perhaps the penultimate act in her short-lived stint as a social worker had been an inspired one after all.

15

The key to getting away with something in a house full of nosy foster siblings is to appear bored, and entirely uninteresting. Marin tucked herself into the corner of the sitting room sofa where she had a view of the front door and also of the phone hanging on the kitchen wall. She flipped through a book in her lap, pretending not to care when her foster mother left the house, slamming the door on her way out. Or when, one by one, all seven of her foster siblings drifted upstairs or onto the front stoop of the old Victorian, or over to the park at the end of the street.

The second they were all gone, however, Marin dashed into the kitchen. She dragged a stool over and kneeled on the vinyl seat cover so she could reach the phone. She tucked the receiver between her ear and shoulder and pulled the folded paper out of her pocket. She punched in the numbers, checking and double-checking each one.

Marin folded the paper and tucked it back into her pocket. She clutched the phone with both hands while the cord twitched anxiously below.

"Pick up, pick up, pick up," Marin whispered.

The third ring was interrupted by a gravelly voice. "Hello?"

Wait. What was she going to say? Marin hadn't thought that far ahead. "Um, can I speak to Talula?"

"Who?"

"Talula Walter. She used to—"

"Wrong number."

Click.

Marin sank onto her heels. Talula was her only lead.

A chill crept over the girl's skin. Those old houses, at least the ones that haven't been shored up over the years, are drafty, creaking structures. So the air that dampened the back of Marin's neck could've come from a window banging open at the rear of the house, or from a particularly vengeful breeze pushing through the widening gaps between door and frame.

The phone in her hand began beeping and she

hung it up. Around the edges of the phone, and along the seams that stretched from floor to ceiling, the kitchen wallpaper peeled away, revealing a dismal yellow beneath.

Marin squeezed her eyes shut. She was out of ideas and out of time.

In that moment, it felt like the little trapdoor of hope that she'd always kept propped open had been kicked shut, and locked, with a big old boulder rolled over the top of it. It felt like that boulder was on top of her shoulders, squashing her chest, making it hard to breathe, and hard to think and hard to move a single muscle.

"What are you doing in here?"

Marin slipped off the stool and stumbled to catch her balance. Becky. Of course. "Nothing."

"You're not supposed to use the telephone. I'm telling."

"Go ahead." Marin slid past the other girl. It didn't matter if she got in trouble with her foster mother. Ms. Blackbourne was going to introduce her to someone who wanted to be her permanent mother any day now.

But what if Marin hadn't given up yet on the one she already had? What if she didn't want a new mother? There had to be another way to track down Talula. Marin would just have to find it.

16

Gilda Blackbourne was not a woman easily intimidated. She didn't blink when called to stand toe-to-toe with an officer of the law who saw the execution of that law being carried out, shall we say, differently than Gilda herself. She did not balk at entering a building scarred with bullet holes and infested with cockroaches. But as she stood before the glass facade of Dr. Lucy Chang's apartment building, her toes began to curl inside her shoes.

The doorman was kind enough, whisking her in through the revolving doors and obligingly pressing the elevator button for her with a white-gloved finger. "The doctor is expecting you, Ms. Blackbourne," he said. The elevator was flawless—it didn't whine or shimmy one bit while it climbed upward. The whole thing made Gilda feel scruffy and underdressed.

As the light illuminating the floor number flashed steadily higher, Gilda gathered her composure. She was in charge here. She would not be intimidated. She had a job to do. The elevator stopped on the top floor. There was a single apartment on the top floor.

The elevator dinged as it slid open to reveal a small hallway with just two doors—one leading to the stairwell, and one with a brass *P* for penthouse above the doorbell. Even the hallway was elegant, with lofty, skylit ceilings.

Dr. Lucy, as it turned out, possessed a smile as lovely as her name. The crisp ends of Lucy's black hair swished against her silk blouse as she beckoned Gilda inside. The social worker stepped over the threshold and her heels plunged into the plush carpet. Oh, how nice it would feel to sink her tired feet into the soft fibers, to strip off her stockings and set her toes free. But she would not be wooed—not by the carpet, or by the rich woodwork, and certainly not by the tall windows opening to a view of the fog-drenched bay.

"Would you like some water? Or some juice? I could make a pot of coffee, but honestly, I drink so much at the hospital, I may as well wheel an IV bag full of the stuff around with me; I try to stick to tea at home. But I could make you a cup of coffee if you want." Lucy bit her lip to keep from saying more.

Gilda tried not to take comfort in the doctor's clear discomfort. Really, she tried. "Is so much glass a safe building practice in this part of California?"

"Absolutely. The unit was certified earthquake-ready by the city, and all the windows are safety glass. Please, have a look around."

Gilda peered into the kitchen. Cleaning supplies—locked up. Knives—out of reach. The dining table was set for two; one of the settings glistened as if it had just been rinsed, while the other was beginning to gather dust. The living room was sparsely furnished, the couch and armchairs pivoted to face an enclosed gas fireplace with a large framed print over the mantel.

"That's lovely," Gilda remarked. After all, professional didn't have to mean unfriendly.

"Oh, thank you! My grandmother was an accomplished calligrapher."

Gilda edged away from Dr. Lucy's open smile. She showed herself down the narrow hallway and to the bathrooms, the doctor's bedroom, and the office. Finally, she thrust back her shoulders and stood before the last door, the one with a cut-crystal doorknob. Gilda Blackbourne was objective, rational, and impartial. She would not be wooed. She would not.

Gilda opened the door and walked in. The walls were empty. The drawers in the little dresser were empty. The closet with a bright light overhead (the cord had been extended so a child might reach it) was empty too. The twin bed was crisply made, the sheets still creased from the packaging they came in. The whole room was empty. Waiting.

Gilda felt a shift in the plush carpet and turned to see Dr. Lucy leaning against the door frame. Her eyes rested on the open dresser drawers and her lips turned down at the edges. Gilda's resolve faded, just a little.

Dr. Lucy sniffed, once, and straightened. "Would you like to see anything else?"

"No, thank you," Gilda said. "But perhaps I will have that cup of tea."

The social worker bobbed the tea bag inside her mug with her left hand while her right printed tiered notes on a yellow steno pad. Dr. Lucy sat across from her, eyes purposely averted so it wouldn't seem as if she were trying to read Gilda's writing.

Gilda cleared her throat. She was down to her last question, the most important one. "What makes you the right foster-adopt candidate for Marin Greene?"

The doctor set her teacup down and trailed her

fingertips over her lips. "I want to be the right candidate. But I can't say definitively whether I am or not."

She leaned forward, planting her elbows on the tabletop and lifting the teacup once more. But instead of drinking, her head ticked to the side. "Every so often, we get a case at the hospital that one single doctor, with her own area of specialty or generality, can't find the answer to. It's a riddle that needs more than one head to be solved. We come together, a whole conference room packed full of experts." The skin around Dr. Lucy's eyes crinkled. "We have, perhaps, more resources than Child Protective Services. But the results, it seems, are the same. Sometimes if we think hard enough, and out-of-the-box enough, we find a solution. Other times, all the brains we can muster still can't solve the problem."

Gilda looked up from her notes and clicked her pen closed.

Lucy took a sip of her tea and swirled the leaves in the bottom of her cup. "It's up to you to decide whether I'm the right candidate for Marin. Maybe, much as I'd like to be, I'm not."

17

At promptly three o'clock on a chilly Wednesday, Marin and her social worker arrived at a little park in the middle of the city to meet Lucy. The grass was green and the sky was gray, with occasional glimpses of almost-blue peering through the thick sheet of clouds.

"She's a doctor?" Marin asked, though she'd already been told the answer.

"Yes." Gilda patted the girl's shoulder. "She's very nice. And not a smarty-pants for how smart she is."

"She wants to adopt me?"

"If the two of you are a good match, then yes, she does."

Marin watched as Dr. Lucy Chang approached.

The woman was nervous—that much was obvious. She kept lifting a finger to her lips, nibbling at a cuticle, and then shoving her hands back into her pockets.

Well, good. Marin was nervous too.

"Hello, Gilda. Hello, Marin," Lucy said. "It's great to see you both."

Marin didn't answer. All those years in the foster system, she had believed that if she stayed still enough, if she was quiet enough, her mother couldn't help but see how easy it would be to take her daughter back. Marin had spent years perfecting a wispy-thin, quiet-as-a-mouse exterior. And it wouldn't do her a bit of good now, not if, before she had a chance to even talk to her mother, to even try to convince her, some other woman swooped in to take her place.

No, what she needed now was the opposite of that invisible girl. She needed to be the kind of girl no one would ever want to adopt. So she didn't smile. She didn't say hello. And she squashed any sympathy she might have felt for the doctor until it was small as a pebble she could stamp into the ground beneath her heel.

18

Every so often, people in the bustling city of San Francisco would cast their arms out to the side and hold very still as the ground beneath them groaned. It wasn't that the earth below wanted to disrupt the city above, but it couldn't help it, you see.

Some things in this world are meant to move. Some things simply cannot hold still, no matter how they try.

A tectonic plate is meant to shift. And so, shift it does.

19

If you were leaving tomorrow, and you had to pack up everything you owned, what would you need? A trunk? A RocketBox? A U-Haul?

Everything Marin owned fit inside a single suitcase. In fact, everything fit inside with room to spare. A few changes of clothes, the piggy bank wrapped in her pajamas, and her copy of the *I Ching*. The pennies, as always, traveled in her pocket. There were the sheets she slept in, of course, but they didn't belong to her. The towels, the comb, the shampoo—not hers, either. Every once in a while a Christmas or birthday gift would arrive from a charity organization, sometimes still bearing the tag: GIRL, AGES 9–12. But she rarely took those things with her when she left. More often than not, they smelled funny, like pity.

Marin's foster mother was upstairs that minute, changing the sheets on her bunk bed for the girl who would take her place. Marin hadn't said good-bye to the other kids in the house, though they watched her step carefully down the staircase, some with longing in their eyes and others with jealousy.

Marin closed the door behind her and waited on the steps of the old Victorian. She had thought Ms. Blackbourne would arrive in a car, but instead she watched the woman cross the street and stride down the sidewalk. The social worker was wearing a skirt and a button-down shirt under a blazer. And panty hose with ankle socks pulled over the top, inside bright pink tennis shoes. Marin didn't like the idea of panty hose in tennis shoes, though she tried to wipe her disapproval from her face.

"Well?" Gilda said when she arrived at the bottom of the stairs, huffing a little.

"We're not driving there?" Marin eyed her suitcase. It wasn't that heavy, not if you only had to carry it a few blocks.

"Your new placement is just a cable car ride away." Gilda attempted to sneak a little extra sunshine into her voice. Marin hated it when adults did that—tried to make you think something was more fun than it actually was. Usually that meant there was something nasty coming—a needle in the arm or a pop quiz or a visit to the dentist's chair.

Marin hefted her suitcase. She had to lean away from it a little, so it didn't scrape against the pavement as she walked. Gilda led the way down the street and around the corner.

Marin had wrapped the piggy bank carefully, and made sure the clasp had clicked when she closed the suitcase, but she didn't trust the old thing not to bust open, scattering her clothes on the street and cracking the piggy bank on the sidewalk like Humpty Dumpty. So she held on with both hands the whole way there, even though it made her walk in sort of a drag-shuffle way.

They climbed aboard the cable car and Marin set down her suitcase at last. Her face was hot and her skin clammy despite the chill in the air. She peeled her cardigan off her shoulders and double-knotted it around her waist. She held on, one hand on her suitcase and the other on the pole as the topsy-turvy thing ambled down the street.

The fog had left them. At the top of the hill you could just see it way out on the ocean, a thin gray line hunkered down and waiting for the winds or the barometer or the night to usher it back over the bay.

By the time they stepped off the cable car, Marin and Gilda may as well have been in a different city entirely. The cloudy sky was the same, and the hills, hills, hills were the same. But rather than block after block of old buildings still peeling away the bright paint of their younger years, everything here shot straight up to the sky. The sidewalks were busy with people stamping determinedly up and down the city blocks.

Gilda stopped in front of a tall apartment building. "Here we are!" Again, the extra dose of cheerfulness. Gilda reached into her large purse and pulled out the same pair of slightly scuffed heels from the other day. She yanked off her shoes and socks and wedged her feet inside the heels with a grunt.

"This is just a trial, remember," Gilda said when she noticed that her slight companion wasn't soaking up any of the cheer. "If it's not a good match, you don't have to stay."

Marin squinted at the sheets of glass rising up, up, up. The gray sky wiggled and glinted off the windows.

"Safety glass, all of it," Gilda assured her.

20

Owl watched the little girl and the woman with the frizzy globe of hair walk into the tall glass building opposite the bent stovepipe where he lived. Yes, he could see in the dark, and yes, he could look behind himself with a seemingly boneless swivel of his head, but having lived with humans for nearly his whole life, Owl had learned to detect subtler things as well.

The slight girl did not waver in her footsteps behind the other woman, nor did she glance wistfully over her shoulder. But it seemed almost as if the suitcase was dragging her down the sidewalk and inside the spinning glass doors, and not the other way around.

Owl clicked his beak. What terrible thing waited behind all that glass to threaten the hatchling so?

OOOOoooo, Owl thought. *OOOOoooo*.

21

Gilda was always nervous when she dropped a child off at a new home. Whether the introduction went peacefully, or whether it ended in tantrums, she was going to have to leave at the end of it and hope things would sort themselves out. The paperwork had been filed, the procedures had been followed; barring catastrophe, there was no going back now.

Beside her in the elevator, the small girl stared at the floor, two hands gripping her suitcase. She didn't look particularly happy. Maybe she was nervous.

When they reached the top floor, Lucy invited them in to the living room. Lucy watched Marin, Marin stared out the window, and Gilda looked back and forth between the two while she rattled off her list of things that must be said at the beginning of a foster-adopt arrangement.

She finished her speech, not sure at all whether either person had listened to a word she'd said. But her duty had been discharged, so the three of them walked to the bedroom waiting for Marin.

Lucy smoothed her skirt against her hips, then clasped her hands in front of her. Then her hands unclasped again and she crossed her arms, bringing one thumb up to her mouth, where she proceeded to tear at the cuticle with her teeth.

Marin walked over to the bed and laid the suitcase on the white bedspread while the adults paused in the doorway, watching, but not intruding further into her space. Marin shook out her hands and stretched her fingers wide as they would go. She'd never had a room of her own before.

Marin clicked open the clasps and lifted the suitcase lid until the whole thing lay flat like a locket baring its treasures. She unwrapped her pajamas from around the piggy bank, picked it up, and shook it once. The lone coin jangled inside. Marin set it on top of the dresser and stepped back, then forward again to shift it to the side just slightly, until it was perfectly centered on the distressed white dresser top, like a shrine waiting to be adored.

From the doorway, Lucy leaned in toward the social worker and murmured, "What do you think—is she taking this okay?"

"We'll find out soon enough," Gilda answered, just as quietly.

Marin folded each item of clothing and laid it in a drawer. She slid the *I Ching* and her three pennies into her pockets. She tucked the suitcase into the closet and shut the door.

The room was still bare: white walls, white bedposts, white sheets. But it was no longer waiting. There was an occupant, however slight, however reluctant. And with her, frail as it may have been, came hope.

Lucy blinked a second time. "Well, then, how about some games? Or books? I didn't want to guess what you might like and get it wrong, so instead—"

"Why don't you have a husband?" It was an exceedingly rude question to ask. Marin knew that. But she was trying very hard to be rude. And this lady just kept being nice to her, no matter what she did. So she'd had to up her game.

Dr. Lucy set down her fork and pressed her napkin against her lips. "Well, I had someone whom I really loved. And she loved me, too. But the ground shook terribly one day, as it does sometimes, and she didn't make it out of a building that collapsed."

Turns out when you try to be mean to somebody, you're the one who ends up feeling rotten on the inside. "Oh. Well, maybe you'll meet somebody else." Marin shoveled a forkful of rice into her mouth so she couldn't say anything else, mean or otherwise.

Dr. Lucy tilted her head to the side. "A heart is divided into four chambers. There's a left ventricle and a right ventricle, a right atrium and a left atrium. Students of medicine will tell you all about the functions of each part, pumping blood in and out, constricting and releasing. And all that's true—but I also like to think each chamber is responsible for a different kind of love. One for family. One for friends.

22

There is nothing quieter than having dinner wi
someone you don't want to get to know. S
smiles at you, and you do your best to keep your sco
in place. She says nice things, and you try as hard
you can to say something mean in return.

"Should we paint your bedroom?" Lucy asked.

Marin shrugged and pushed the rice on her pl
into a mound with a steep crater in the center.

"Well, what colors do you like best?"

"It doesn't matter."

Lucy blinked. "Maybe wallpaper would be bei
then. Should we go pick some out tomorrow? An
rug, or some posters?"

"Why would I want a rug on carpet?"

Maybe another for pets and really special teachers or something.

"Anyway, she filled up my whole chamber for romantic love. It's still full of her, all these years later. There's no room for anyone else."

Marin scraped her fork against her plate, pushing the pile of peas into wiggly rows. Her plan had backfired. Utterly. The very last thing she meant to do was to feel sorry for Dr. Lucy—that would make it ten times harder to be mean to her. Marin scowled at her peas, but not, perhaps, for the reason Dr. Lucy may have thought.

Lucy picked up her fork again and speared a cube of roasted zucchini. "But the other three chambers of my heart still have lots of room left—the family chamber, and the friends one, and the one for pets, too. What about you? Do you have any room left? Not in the chamber you have saved for your mother, of course. But what about the pet one? Do you think we could make room for a cat to live here with us?"

23

What will be the outcome of finding my mother's old friend Talula Walter? It wasn't the first time Marin had asked, but she was hoping for a different answer this time.

Marin shook the three pennies in her cupped palms and dropped them on top of her desk. Two tails and a head. She consulted the chart in her small book and drew a broken line on a piece of paper. Marin gathered the pennies back into her hand and asked again, shaking them onto the desk a second time.

Eventually, five more lines joined the first on her paper. Marin studied the hexagram. She knew this one. She didn't even have to look it up in her little book. *Youthful folly.*

At least the *I Ching* had a sense of humor.

There are some children who, when issued a warning, will curl up under their blankets and pull their pillows over their heads and stay there until all sign of danger has passed. Marin was most decidedly not one of those.

24

The next day was little better. Lucy complimented the piggy bank, and Marin huffed. Lucy inquired about the *I Ching*, and Marin pretended like she didn't hear the question. Lucy suggested they ask another kid from the building over to play or that they go out for some fresh air. But Marin would not budge.

Quiet filled the afternoon and bounced back and forth in the widening space between them. When a call for Dr. Lucy came in from the hospital, Marin crept into her bedroom and closed the door.

Lucy had given Marin her own phone for emergencies, but Marin had another purpose in mind for the device. Just because the phone number for her mother's friend hadn't worked, that didn't mean Marin couldn't find her. With a few clicks and swipes, she discovered that there were twenty-six Talulas listed online in Northern California. Marin started at the top, and dialed each one. By the fourth call, she had her introduction down.

"Hello, may I speak with Talula please?" And when someone answered in the affirmative: "This is (insert fake name) with the law offices of (more made-up names). Did you ever know a woman by the name of Summer Greene?"

Of course, she asked this in her most gruff, most adult-sounding voice. Some people sounded confused when they answered, and others irritated. Some didn't even respond; they just hung up. Others dithered: "Well, I did know someone named Summer, but she was definitely a Krezmarzick, not a Greene." One woman was so pleased to have a live body on the other end of the line that Marin lost a half an hour of investigative time to an account of the woman's prizewinning peonies and the aphid infestation that had them drooping and listless all spring.

It wasn't until the seventeenth phone call that something interesting happened. The call was picked up on the first ring.

"Lulu's Flower Shop."

"May I speak with Talula, please?"

"No one calls me that anymore. Who is this? I'm not buying."

"Huh? I mean, this is Rhonda Finkelstein with the law offices of Reese, Rolo, and York. Did you know a woman by the name of Summer Greene?"

"Why do you ask—Rhonda, is it?"

"Oh, um, we are just putting some documents, in, um, order and we need to update our files with the correct contact information."

"What if I don't want you to have my contact information?"

"Well, you see, it really would help us if you would just tell me—"

"Marin, is that you?"

Marin threw the phone down on the bedspread. She could still hear Talula talking on the other end of the line. Marin reached down with a shaking finger and hung up the call.

25

reat news," Lucy announced as she set two bowls of clam chowder on the table. "I found a sitter to stay with you while I'm at the hospital."

Marin froze, a spoonful of oyster crackers dunked in soup halfway to her mouth. "I'm not a baby. I don't need a babysitter."

"Of course not," Lucy said as she scooted her chair in and draped a napkin across her lap. "It would just make me feel better to know you're not alone all day. Besides, we're on probation, you and me. I have to demonstrate that you're safe here." She scooped up a few spears of asparagus and stacked them along the edge of her bowl. "And you have to decide if you want to stay."

Marin shoved the crackers into her mouth. They were so soggy, she didn't even have to chew. She gulped down the pulpy hexagons and shoved another spoonful into her mouth. Mushy crackers were better than telling this nice lady that Marin was doing everything she could to make sure she would never stay here.

"Besides," Dr. Lucy said, "you'll like her. Alice just finished her first year of pre-med, so if you want to be left alone, I'm sure she'll be happy to spend all day prepping for her fall classes. On the other hand, if you want a buddy to take you out and do something fun, I'm sure she'll be just as happy for the study break."

26

The "sitter," as Lucy called her, was a punky nineteen-year-old named Alice. When she talked, a ring pierced through her nose as if she were a Spanish bull hovered above her lips. Her head was nearly shaved on both sides and what hair she had left was bright purple.

This girl was supposed to make Marin feel *safer*?

"All right, then, I'll be going," Lucy said, and she pulled the corner of her lip through her teeth. She lifted the strap of her purse over her shoulder and took a step toward the door, only to turn back again. "Maybe I should take the rest of the week off. Give you some time to get used to the place."

"I'm fine," Marin said. "Really."

"You're sure?"

"I have your cell number and your work number and Gilda Blackbourne's number and all the other emergency contacts you programmed in here." Marin held up her phone.

"And I'll be home for lunch."

"And you'll be home for lunch."

"But are you sure—"

"Yes."

Lucy's smile was more of a grimace. "I'm new at this. Be patient with me."

Marin clamped her heart shut. If Dr. Lucy were anyone else—a teacher, a neighbor, an aunt—Marin wouldn't even try to stop herself, she would adore her. But Marin didn't have that luxury. Right now, she couldn't let any other kind of mother in.

Dr. Lucy left, for real this time, and while Alice settled herself on the couch and flipped through an anatomy textbook, Marin ran to the window. If she pressed her cheek against the glass, she could see straight down to the sidewalk, twelve stories below. Before long, the doctor pushed through the swirling door and began the hike up the hill to the hospital. She stopped at the corner, crossed the street, and then turned back to look up at the window. A grin broke over her face and she waved, her whole body rocking back and forth as her arm swept over her head.

Before she could stop herself, Marin waved in return. Before she could bite down to keep it from spreading, a matching grin pulled at her lips.

27

So what do you want to do today?" Alice asked, her nose ring jiggling. Did people's nostrils always move when they talked? And why was Marin just now noticing this? "A picnic at the park? A trip to the children's museum?"

Well, at least Alice was going to make this easy on her. Marin forced herself to look away from the nose ring. She spoke around a mouthful of granola. "Actually, I want to go to the flower shop."

"Okay. That's a little random, but I'm game."

Marin lifted the bowl to her lips and gulped down the last of her milk. If she had to have a babysitter tagging along everywhere she went (even though she wasn't a baby), at least she got one who would go along with whatever she wanted.

28

An owl's eyes are often half lidded during the day. Don't be fooled into thinking that means he's sleepy. Below the sunshade of his upper eyelid, that owl is alert as could be.

Thus, Owl watched the small girl, bones as slender and light as any bird's, make her way down two blocks from the apartment and around the corner. An older girl, bright-plumed as a toucan, followed several steps behind.

Owl ruffled his feathers as they veered out of sight. And odd pair, those two, striding together, but not truly together at all. Owl shifted his weight from one foot to the other and burbled softly to himself. What did it matter? It wasn't up to him to look after the well-being of every wingless hatchling that walked the streets below his perch.

OOOOoooo, he thought. *OOOOoooo. Silence is a true friend who never betrays.*

29

Outside Lulu's Flower Shop, Marin paused with her hand on the door. "You can wait here," she said to Alice. "I'll just be a minute."

"Uh—I think I should go in with you."

"No. I'm working on a surprise for Lucy, and nobody can know about it, not even you." Marin looked straight into Alice's eyes, willing the older girl to believe her.

"Well . . ."

"You can watch me through the window. I'll be right inside."

"I guess. If you're sure."

"I'm sure."

The bell chimed as Marin swung through the

door. A woman sat on a stool behind the counter, one leg crossed over the other, her golden hair braided and knotted and twisted in long, curving clumps. She eyed Marin and pulled a trio of pearl-tipped pins from her lips.

"I wondered when I'd see you."

Marin wasn't going to let this woman startle her anymore. She crossed the black-and-white-checkered tile floor. "I'm Marin. You're Talula. You knew my mother, Summer Greene."

Talula twisted green floral tape around the cut stems of a daylily boutonniere as she eyed the girl in front of her. Why, when this child was concerned, was it always so hard to know right from wrong? "Yes, I knew your mother."

"I have questions."

"I'm sure you do." Talula stuck a pin through the coil of floral tape.

Marin sighed. "Look, I just want to know a little bit about her. I deserve that much."

"I suppose that's true." Talula set the flowers down with a sigh. "Did you know that your mother called you Marin because she was born just north of here in Marin County, and you were born in Marin County, and it was her favorite place in the whole world?"

Talula folded her arms across her chest. Her eyes

drifted to the ceiling as she sifted through memories she hadn't visited in years. "I guess it can't hurt to tell you that Summer loved this city almost as much as she loved Marin County—the fog and the old houses, the hills and the Golden Gate. We used to go down to Lost Weekend when the weather was nasty on our days off and rent old movies—anything with Katharine Hepburn in it—and stay inside all day long.

"But she loved the coast north of here most of all. She went out every year on her birthday to this cliff by the sea. And she'd take all her wishes from the year before—all these little scraps of paper—and throw them into the ocean."

This was not going like Marin had planned. "That's not—look, I get to ask the questions. You were there the day she left."

Talula's focus snapped out of memory and back to the girl standing in front of her. "Oh, honey, I hoped you were too young to remember that."

Marin's lower lip trembled. Her voice shook. "She left me with you. She told you to take care of me. Why didn't you do what she said? Then when she was ready, she could have come back to get me. She just didn't know where to find me for so long, and now she must think it's too late. If you would have just kept me—"

"Honey, when your mother left you with me, I was

in a band that traveled to festivals all up and down the West Coast. We slept on the road between gigs in a Volkswagen bus that smelled like feet and broke down every time we had to go up anything bigger than an anthill. That was no life for a small child. I couldn't keep you."

"Then why didn't she leave me with someone who could, if all she needed was a break?"

Talula leaned forward and clamped her hands on the edge of the counter. "Marin, I don't know why your mother did any of the things she did. And I don't believe in making something up just to make you feel better, no matter that you're only a kid. So listen up.

"Your mother didn't need a break. She needed a new life. I'm sorry. You deserve better than that, but it's the truth, and at the very least someone should tell you."

The coolers that lined the back wall of the flower shop shut off with a fizz and a click. The fluorescent lights inside flickered. Marin backed away from the counter. Maybe if she was quiet enough, then Talula wouldn't see the tears flooding her eyes. She wouldn't know that the breath had stopped moving in and out of Marin's chest.

In fact, Talula didn't see those things. But not because the girl had been rendered invisible; because her own eyes were squeezed shut. She felt that there were some truths a person couldn't say while looking another person in the eyes. Not if one was going to have the courage to finish telling what had to be told.

"Marin, your mother never came back." Talula blew out a long, slow breath. "I made sure that no matter where I traveled, she knew where I was. I made sure I always knew where you were. And she never, not once, came back for you."

Marin may as well have been invisible. When Talula opened her eyes, the shop was empty. Only the tinkling of the bell above the door confirmed that the girl had ever been there.

30

To someone who has never been discarded by a mother, it might not make sense. But for Marin, hearing that Summer Greene didn't now and hadn't ever wanted to be her mother didn't lessen the desire to find her. If anything, it changed it from a whisper-to-yourself-in-the-darkness sort of wish to a hunger that swallows a person whole.

Tracking down someone who doesn't want to be found is no simple thing. Of course Marin tried searching for her mother's name and checking online census records and the Social Security Administration database and high school reunion meet-up boards across the state. But Marin's birth mother was an off-the-grid kind of person. If Talula was to be believed, she was a float-from-one-life-to-the-other, drift-from-one-obsession-to-another, wander-from-one-place-to-another kind of person.

Truth be told, sometimes in the loneliest, most sleepless nights, Marin wondered if Summer was even her mother's real name. Sometimes she wondered if she was ever going to find her.

But when the fog of hurt around Talula's words began to dissipate, Marin discovered something hidden there. A real something. One place her mother went every year on her birthday, to a cliff in Marin County to scatter her wishes from the past year. But what cliff? And how come Marin didn't even know her mother's birthday?

31

What weighs more—a city, or an ocean? Both press down upon the earth with the ponderous weight of the souls they carry.

Below the leagues of water, below the sand and the skeletons of sunken ships and the bones of creatures who lived and thrashed about and sank to the ocean floor thousands of years ago, the tectonic plates that held it all up groaned. They groaned and stretched and strained against the weight holding them down.

32

The next time the small girl and her birdlike watcher left the whirling glass doors of the apartment building and disappeared again around the corner, Owl did not just ruffle his feathers and burble to himself. Even though the day was bright as bright could be, he shuffled to the edge of the stovepipe, unfurled his dappled wings, and dropped into the air.

He circled once and set off after her. People on the sidewalks below blinked and turned their eyes skyward when his broad shadow passed over them. It went against every feather in his body to be *seen* by so many creatures, but if he had learned one thing from his teacher, it was that when you feel that pull on your feathers, it is best to pay attention.

The girl hadn't gotten far when Owl settled into a glide above her. He pumped his wings once, twice, and floated up to a scrollwork perch in the eaves of a green and yellow Victorian across the street. The old building seemed out of place next to the high-rises and several-story office buildings that sprouted like weeds all around it. Owl preferred the feel of wood beneath his feet, and anyway, the modern buildings more often than not had spikes to keep avian guests away.

Owl watched the pair pick their way along the sidewalk. He had tried, in the years since his teacher had died, to keep up with his daily study. But without a teacher, he sometimes found that he needed to travel far afield, and to look for learning in unconventional places.

OOOOoooo, Owl thought. *OOOOoooo. By three methods we may learn wisdom: first, by reflection, which is noblest; second, by imitation, which is easiest; and third, by experience, which is the bitterest.*

33

Marin did not see the round eyes blinking at her from high above as she left Alice outside and disappeared once again into the flower shop. Talula was with a customer, so Marin strolled through the aisles of cut flowers waiting to be chosen. She leaned in to sniff a few, and drew her fingers across the waxy leaves of others.

But she wasn't here for flowers. Answers—that's what she wanted.

When the bell clanged and the shop emptied, Marin strode to the counter and propped her elbows against the glass.

Talula sighed. "Marin, I really don't think you should be here."

Marin screwed up her face. "You said Summer went to a cliff every year. Which one?"

"*Marin,*" Talula began carefully. "I don't think I should be answering those kinds of questions. In fact, I think I should call your social worker and tell her you've been coming here." Talula frowned. "Where did I put that paper with her number on it?"

"She already knows."

Of course, that was a lie. But a girl doesn't stand a chance in the foster care system if she can't spin a little yarn from time to time. Eyes full forward. No blinking. Look bored. Marin leaned her chin against her fist and kicked a leg out behind her.

"My social worker is going with me. We're going to say good-bye to Summer on that cliff."

"Marin, what are you doing? Summer doesn't want to be found."

"Yeah, well, she won't actually *be* there when we go, just the *idea* of her, someplace important to her. I have to say good-bye before I can get adopted. You know—for closure. It's part of the process."

Talula chewed on the inside of her cheek. "Honestly, I don't know which cliff she went to. But she said something about the place being fitting, seeing as how her life was like one big shipwreck."

"Oh." Marin slid away from the counter and back

toward the door. She was just reaching for the handle when Talula spoke one more time.

"For what it's worth, you're doing the right thing, letting her go."

The air outside was wet and crisp, but it couldn't cool the heat in Marin's cheeks. That lady didn't know anything. Not what Marin needed. Not what Summer wanted. Talula was just one more person in the long chain of adults who'd passed Marin along because looking out for her was too inconvenient.

She didn't know anything.

34

A knock sounded on Marin's bedroom door.

"Just a minute!" She swept her three pennies and the scrap of paper with the half-cast hexagram under her pillow and shoved her pocket-size *I Ching* in after them. She scrambled over to the foot of the bed and sat primly on the edge.

"Come in."

Dr. Lucy peered inside. "I'm making some tea. Would you like some?"

Marin shook her head.

"Apple slices? With peanut butter and raisins?"

"No, thank you."

Lucy leaned her hip against the door frame. "Should we go hunting for shells on the beach? Or up into the hills—we could go for a hike?"

Still, the girl shook her head.

"To Disneyland? To Paris? To the moon?"

Marin lifted a hand over her mouth to stop her laughter.

"You know, Marin, I think maybe you and I should get something out of the way."

Marin sat up even straighter.

"I don't want to take your mother's place. I'm sure she must be very important to you. But I hope that doesn't mean you and I can't become a little family of our own. You know that's what I want, don't you? I want it more than anything. But not unless that's what you want too."

Marin squirmed and wedged her hands under her legs.

"Sometimes at the hospital we have to do operations on kids even younger than you if one of their organs doesn't work the way it's supposed to. Like a kidney, for example." Lucy twisted around so she could outline the space between her spine and her ribs where a kidney belongs.

"Kidneys have an essential job. A person can't live without her kidneys. But sometimes, for whatever reason, an organ can't perform its essential tasks, no matter how hard it works and no matter how much it might want to.

"So a new one takes its place. One that's ready to do its job so the kid can get better." Lucy nodded, satisfied with her explanation.

"Try not to think of me as your new mother, Marin. Think of me as a new kidney, just ready to do this new job I've been given." She took hold of the doorknob and began to pull it closed. "If you'll let me, that is."

35

A word can be overused.

Magnificent, for example. What a word! But if your sandwich is magnificent, and your trip to the hardware store is magnificent, and your ride on a roller coaster is magnificent, then doesn't everything tied to that word become a little less, well, magnificent?

And what about *mother*?

Seven women had borne that name for Marin. Her mother, first, and then each of the foster "mothers" who had come after. If they were all her mothers, in a way, then what did that word even mean? A person who brings you into the world? A person who gives you a place to stay if you're not too difficult? A person who takes you in so she can pay the bills?

What would it be like to have a real mother? Not a biological one or a temporary one, but one who chose the job, who wanted the work, who fought for the right to bear that title. What would it be like, Marin wondered, to have a mother who wanted her?

36

Owl should have been sleeping. It's what any sensible Strigidae would do during the daylight hours. But instead he found himself flicking an eye open every time the glass doors at the ground level of the apartment building across the street began to whirl, depositing a pedestrian or two on the sidewalk.

Ninety-nine times out of a hundred, it wasn't her. But when the slight girl emerged, Owl's pinfeathers would bristle with purpose and he'd chase the sleep from his head with a ruffling shake. Except—

There she was, walking out the doors and up the sidewalk. The older girl walked beside her, matching her stride for stride. They crossed at the crosswalk and continued on together, headed for the park, or the botanical gardens, or the bay. Actually together. They walked side by side. They even laughed as they talked.

OOOOoooo, Owl crooned. *OOOOoooo*.

Perhaps the little hatchling didn't need him looking out for her. Perhaps it was time to return to the forest, to the misty heights of the redwood trees, where he belonged. After all, no one needed him here. Not anymore.

37

That night, when Lucy knocked on Marin's door and peeked in, she caught a glimpse of the small book tucked under Marin's leg.

"You know," Lucy said, "my grandmother consulted the *I Ching* every day, but I never learned how. Will you show me?"

Marin nodded cautiously and lifted the book onto her lap. She pulled her three pennies out of her pocket and handed them to Lucy.

"You have to think of a question and say it out loud."

"Okay. Will we find a cure for cancer?"

"No, that's too general. You have to pick something specific."

"Hmmm. Should we get a cat?"

Marin almost smiled, but she caught herself just in time. "That will work. Now ask your question and throw the coins."

"Should Marin and I get a cat?" Lucy asked aloud, and she shook the pennies onto the desk. Together they leaned in to look.

"Two heads and a tail," Marin announced. She opened her little book to the index page and marked a single line. "Again."

Lucy asked her question and tossed the pennies twice more. Marin marked two more lines, each above the last. She pointed with the eraser to the block of three lines. "This is the lower trigram." She peered into her book. "*Ch'ien.* It means heaven. Go again, three more times."

Lucy obeyed, and Marin dutifully scratched her marks each time. Lucy watched as the girl beside her squinted at the result. Her lips moved soundlessly as she counted, and her eyes flicked up as she sorted the dashes and lines into blocky groups.

"The upper trigram is *K'an,* or water. Together they make the hexagram *Hsu,* or calculated waiting." Marin flipped to the correct page in her little book and held her place with a finger. She looked up into Dr. Lucy's face. "Do you want me to read your answer to you?"

"Please."

Marin cleared her throat. "The cosmos indicates a period of waiting, like when observing a cloud that has yet to give forth rain, for great change is underway...."

Lucy might have laughed at the mention of the cosmos—she was, after all, a woman of science. She didn't believe in divination. She believed in the physics of blood moving through vessels and the engineering of bones and their joints, and the religion of the scientific method.

But Marin took her task so very earnestly that Lucy stuffed down any skepticism she might have held and listened. She didn't understand this girl—what made her so solemn, so determined not to settle in. Lucy didn't yet understand, but she wanted to. Desperately.

38

Gilda arrived at Dr. Lucy's apartment for their first postplacement visitation and knocked just as the second hand of her wristwatch clicked twelve. When the door swung open, Lucy, and her smile, and her sleek black hair, and her perfect silk blouse, greeted Gilda. A pot of steeping tea and two mugs waited on the dining room table.

Gilda marched across the carpet. She would not be wooed. She would not. "We'll speak separately. The child is in her room?"

"Yes."

Gilda sat and opened the file before her while Lucy poured the tea. Gilda pulled out a clean sheet of paper and uncapped her pen. Date, time, case number 014563. As she waited for Lucy to sit, the tip of her pen hovered expectantly over the page.

"And how are you both doing?"

"Fine. We're fine. Marin's quiet. She keeps to herself, but I wouldn't say she's unhappy."

"And you?"

Lucy's slim shoulders shot up and slowly settled back down again. "I'm new at this. I don't know enough to even know what I'm not doing right."

"You're back to work? Life is carrying on as usual?"

"Yes. I have a sitter who stays with Marin while I'm gone."

"Good." Gilda paused while she added a few quick notes with sharp dots beside them. "In these adjustment periods, time apart is just as important as time spent together."

Gilda asked each of the prescribed questions and took notes while Lucy talked. When she had run out of queries, Gilda set her pen down in the long silence that followed. She blew across the surface of her tea and stared at the bits of leaves settling at the base of the porcelain teacup. "It sounds like you're trying," she said finally. "And that you really do want this to work. That matters far more than experience."

"Thank you," Lucy said.

In circumstances such as these, it isn't always easy to know how much to reveal and how much to withhold. There are times when no amount of words can bring a thing into being; times when one's own wishes have no bearing whatsoever. What Lucy wanted was beside the point. It was up to Marin to choose.

"Would you like to speak with Marin now?"

"Yes." Gilda pushed away from the table and moved down the hall to the room with the crystal doorknob. She knocked and, after a few moments of silence, let herself in.

"Hello there, Marin."

The girl sat on her bed, her hands tucked under her legs and her eyes wide. "Hi."

"Is there anything you want to tell me?"

Marin shook her head.

Gilda pulled out the chair at the little white desk and sat down. It wasn't exactly comfortable, as it was made for someone half her size, but Gilda had never had good luck inspiring confidence in children while she towered over them.

"Is there anything I can do to help you?"

Marin's eyes lifted from her lap and stuck on the file in Gilda's hands, but she only shook her head again.

"Do you think you can be happy here?"

Marin scrunched her lips to the side. "Dr. Lucy is nice," she finally said.

"Well. If you think of anything you want to tell me, you have my phone number, correct?" When Marin nodded a third time, Gilda opened the file and began flipping through the stack of documents. "All the papers are in order; your court date is set for two weeks from today."

"All the papers?"

"Yes, indeed. You are now legally free to be adopted. Isn't that great?"

If Gilda Blackbourne's only charge had been a soft-spoken penny-carrying eleven-year-old, the social worker might have noticed that the news didn't bring about quite the joyful reaction she had been hoping for.

But there were dozens of children under Gilda's purview. Some of them ran away from their group homes on a weekly basis. Some had scrapes with the law. Some were so crushed by the failures of the families they were born into that she feared they would never learn how to trust another human being in the whole of their lives.

So hopefully you can forgive Gilda for not noticing Marin's furtive glances at her case file, or how, even in such a bright and welcoming home, the girl sat in a narrow corner at the very tip of her bed. She didn't sink into the pile of pillows or sprawl on the plush carpet. Her room, though she slept there every night, was still empty.

39

Luck is a fickle companion; you never know when it's going to grace you with its presence. Marin took a deep breath and dialed the number for Lost Weekend Video.

"Yes, hello. I would like to pay the outstanding fines on my rental account."

"Name?"

"Summer Greene. With an *e* at the end."

"Card number?"

"I'm afraid I've lost the card. Will the name be sufficient?" Marin held her breath.

"Yeah—I can pull up the record here. Just a sec. . . . I see three unreturned videos from—yikes—July of 2007. Good thing for you we don't charge interest.

You owe $37.98. How would you like to pay?"

"I'll put the money in the mail tomorrow."

"Okay, but you won't be able to check out anything else until the balance has been cleared. Oh, and since the account has been dormant for so long, you'll need to come get a new card and update all your information."

"Um. I don't know if I'll be able to come down to the store this week—can you read me the information you have in the system and I'll let you know if there are updates?"

"I guess. Account holder: Summer Greene. Flagged genres: travel, foreign film, classic cinema."

"Correct. And can you tell me if Talula Walter is still granted privileges on the account?"

"Yep."

"You can take her off. And can you just double-check that my date of birth is correct in the system?" Marin bit down on the corner of her pillow.

"August 14, 1984."

"Yes, that's right. Look for that payment in the mail this week. Thank you!" Marin squeaked, and she hung up the phone.

August 14. But that was only a few days away!

The hair on Marin's arms rose until it stood straight up and a shiver rippled over her skin. Summer could be here, in the city, already. This was what Marin had been waiting for and hoping for all those lonely years. She tried on a smile, but it slipped away again just as quickly.

If what Talula said was true, in five days' time, Summer would be standing on some cliff in Marin County, tossing her wishes into the sea.

40

If Alice had been expecting yet another trip to the flower shop, she didn't object when Marin requested a visit to the library, instead. She'd simply nodded in approval as she began stacking her textbooks inside a brown leather satchel. In went highlighters and index cards and three pencils with very sharp points. When the doors to the library opened promptly at nine, the two of them were waiting.

Marin could have gone straight to the stacks and hunted for a book on California beaches, but this wasn't her first time in a public library. They were good places to kill time when you didn't have any money to spend. And if she had learned one thing in all those lonely afternoons she'd spent at one library or another, it was that a librarian would do just about anything for a kid with a question.

So Marin left Alice at a big study table with her anatomy books spread all around her and her faux hawk bobbing as she flipped through study cards. Marin approached the reference desk.

"Excuse me," she whispered. Extra points for whispering.

The librarian wore bright red lipstick and thick-framed reading glasses that swept upward at the tips. "How can I help you?" she asked, and the red lips curved up, just like the glasses.

"My babysitter made me a scavenger hunt to keep me busy this summer, and I'm stumped on my next clue. I was hoping you could help me."

"Well, I don't want to take the fun out of you figuring it out for yourself!"

Marin leaned in and whispered, "My babysitter is big on the idea of process being just as important as product. So here I am, consulting an expert, and using the resources available to me." Extra-extra points for flattery. "I think asking you is just what she had in mind."

The librarian winked an artfully lined eye. "In that case, what's the clue?"

"I have to find a Marin County beach where there

are shipwrecks in the water. And cliffs. There have to be cliffs, too."

The librarian tapped a pencil against her cheek. "Hmmm. Perhaps we should start with shipwrecks, because there are likely fewer of those than cliffs. Yes?"

Marin nodded.

"Follow me."

The librarian swiveled out of her chair and set off for the reference section. She wove through the stacks like a barrel-racing mare until she found her Dewey-Decimal destination. "Nine-ten point four: accounts of travel, discoveries, shipwrecks, adventure. Do you see any books there on Marin County?"

Marin dropped to the floor so she was eye level with the multicolored spines. There were thick hardbound books with gold-embossed titles next to small tourist guides for the treasure-hunting backpacker. Marin tapped past the books one by one. She didn't get far before she saw her own name on the spine of a thin hardcover.

Marin felt a little shock tingle up her arm. This was why she bore the name she did. This was the thing that would bring her and her mother back together again. It was like a clue given to her on the day she was born and just waiting all these years to be discovered.

Marin pulled the book from the shelf and handed it to the librarian.

"Spot on. And now, California—coast range counties, north."

Finding a book on beaches near San Francisco wasn't difficult. Marin tucked one under her arm and followed the librarian to a table across the room from Alice. The librarian peeked over at the reference desk. No patrons were tapping their fingers on the counter or huffing in her direction, so she leaned in and whispered conspiratorially, "I love scavenger hunts!"

Marin smiled. Perfect. "Maybe you can make a list of all the shipwrecks and I'll make a list of all the beaches with cliffs, and we'll see if we get a match."

While they searched, the fog lifted and the sun streamed in through the library windows, making every bit of bookish dust shimmer and glow. The clock on the wall ticked softly with little other sound to accompany it besides the intermittent whoosh of turning pages.

"Oh, will you look at this one!" the librarian exclaimed.

Marin leaned across the table, resisting the urge to lift her finger to her lips to remind the librarian to keep her voice down. Opposite several dense paragraphs of text was a pen-and-ink drawing of the

SS *Tennessee* listing perilously toward the breakers.

The librarian cleared her throat. "The fog rolled in as the ship steamed toward the mouth of the San Francisco Bay. By the time the fog lifted, the captain realized he was headed not for the port city but into the dark sands of what we know now as Tennessee Cove. You can still see fragments of the rusted engine rising out of the water in the low tide."

Marin leaned closer. There, at the edge of the drawing, were cliffs dropping into the sea. "That's it." She could taste it like copper on her tongue. She knew.

"We should still cross-check the rest just to make sure we're not missing something."

Marin nodded and turned back to her book of beaches. *Tennessee Cove.* She didn't know whether it was from some long-forgotten memory or if the finicky cosmos had finally decided to give her a break. Marin traced the line of cliffs with her fingertip, and a shiver rolled through her. She knew where to go, and when. Now she just had to figure out how to get there.

41

Pressure builds until there is release. The more pressure, the more spectacular the release. Take Old Faithful: a cauldron of water filling so full, it bursts into the sky when the pressure becomes too great.

But along the San Andreas Fault, it isn't a geyser we're talking about. It's two continental plates smashing together.

Sometimes the release is just a little tremor. Other times it's a rumble that makes the ground all around it shiver. In the city above, people pause, move away from the windows and under tables just to be safe. When it passes, they go on about their day, brushing off the quake like dust from their shoulders, and try to forget the dragon sleeping beneath them.

But sometimes the pressure is too much; it builds for too long and the release isn't spectacular at all.

It's terrible.

42

Dr. Lucy Chang had never had children before. She didn't work in a school, or in the pediatric wing of her hospital, and her own nieces and nephews lived on the opposite coast. She only ever saw tantrums in grocery stores and squeals of delight in city parks and orderly lines of uniform-clad schoolchildren filing in and out of the museum down the street from her apartment.

So she can be forgiven, surely, for underestimating the range of emotions Marin might have felt at the thought of losing her only family member in one tap of a judge's gavel, or the lengths her foster child might go to in order to see her mother again.

In fact, the things Lucy didn't know about children

far outweighed the things she did. She didn't know, for example, to keep a stockpile of macaroni and cheese cartons in the cupboard and chicken nuggets in the freezer for the times, like that night, when Marin would not put a single bite of eggplant parmigiana into her mouth. She didn't know that Band-Aids were more for the spirit than the injury. And she had no idea that while she sipped her oak-aged Shiraz and painstakingly layered strips of breaded eggplant and cheese and sauce in a baking dish, Marin was, at that very moment, putting into motion her plan to leave Lucy for good.

43

For Marin's part, she didn't mean to hurt anyone, especially not Lucy, who was kind, and open, and so completely safe. But Marin couldn't afford to worry about that. She had to see her mother.

So while Lucy's back was turned, Marin grabbed the doctor's cell phone out of her purse, scrolled through the contacts list, and typed out a single message.

Marin hid the rest of the night in her room. She couldn't eat a bite of her dinner, not because she was ungrateful, or because she couldn't get past the slimy, chewy, seedy strips of eggplant, but because she knew how much Lucy wanted her to stay.

And yet, rather than excitement or eager anticipation for the day to come, unease hung in the air about her and settled over her skin. Marin opened her little copy of the *I Ching* and pulled her three pennies out of her cardigan pocket. She took a breath and asked: *What will be the outcome of meeting my mother tomorrow?* Six times she cast the pennies; six times she made a mark.

Three solid lines above three broken ones. *Stagnation.* A wrinkle formed on the girl's brow as she read the tiny script. Not *Unity,* or *Prospering,* or even *Grace,* but *Stagnation?*

Another name for the *I Ching* is the *Book of Changes;* if a person isn't ready to face the topsy-turvy changes that come with this life, perhaps she shouldn't choose the *I Ching* as her guide. After all, the ancient book is a reflection of life, and life is anything but stagnant.

44

Lucy must have checked her watch a dozen times. It wasn't like Alice to be late. Lucy had a surgery in thirty minutes and two more that morning stacked on top of one another. She should have left already.

"Go," Marin urged as she stuck a banana in Lucy's purse and practically shoved her foster mother out the door. "I'm sure Alice will be here any minute. It's only just after seven o'clock. We're going to the science museum today and she told me she's really looking forward to it."

"I do need to go, but—"

"I'll be fine."

"You'll call me if you need anything?"

"Promise."

Lucy hesitated, her eyes fixed on Marin's upturned face. How any woman could have left that girl behind was beyond her. She knew she couldn't begin to comprehend how that decision had shattered Marin. Lucy just thanked her lucky stars that she was the one chosen to pick up the pieces.

45

Marin watched through the front windows as Lucy left. She didn't plan to wave, and she certainly didn't plan to smile again, but she couldn't seem to stop herself.

She waited twenty minutes, just in case Lucy forgot something and had to return to the apartment. She checked and double-checked the directions for her route. She drank a glass of water and then worried that she would have to pee and end up missing her bus.

When she couldn't wait any longer, Marin crept down the hallway, down the stairs, across the lobby, beneath the notice of the doorman, and out the swirling doors on feet that barely made more than a whisper of sound as they touched the ground.

The limo driver waiting on the corner might have wondered if she was quite ready to venture out onto the streets of San Francisco alone. The street vendors with their mounds of ripe peaches and avocados, trucked in from orchards inland of the constant chill of the San Francisco fog, might have stopped her and demanded that she give them a phone number to call, just to make sure she was all right. The bike messenger who whizzed past might have slowed to ask if she needed directions. Any one of them might have, but they didn't.

Marin crossed the street to the bus stop. The hiss and slam of the bus brakes startled Owl and he blinked his eyes, well, owlishly. The bus doors opened with a hiss and the girl climbed inside, her hand outstretched so the bus driver could count out the fare in her palm.

The doors closed behind her and the bus shrugged forward. Owl blinked. Hatchlings were not supposed to be unsupervised for too long, and they were definitely not supposed to leave the nest alone. Owl shifted to the very edge of the metal stovepipe. He swiveled his neck and watched the bus swing wide around the corner. Perhaps he was needed after all.

OOOOoooo, Owl burbled. *OOOOoooo*. He opened the wide fan of his wings and leaped from his perch.

46

The bus lumbered through the streets and up and down the hills. Passengers stepped on and off, whisking about their business: elderly women with grocery bags straining under the weight of jars of prune juice and tins of brined fish; buskers with their scarred instrument cases trading one street corner for another; and at one point, an entire preschool class on an outing to the aquarium.

Even though Marin had memorized the route, she sat in the swaying bus uneasily. She didn't like lying to Lucy. She liked everything about Lucy, actually. If she didn't already have a plan—if, for the past seven years, her heart hadn't been latched on to reuniting with her mother—she might let herself admit that she could be happy there, in Lucy's house.

When it was time to transfer, Marin gripped the pole by her seat as the bus lurched to a stop. She scrambled down the stairs and onto the sidewalk. The wheel wells reached nearly as high as her shoulders and the exhaust burned her eyes. She hurried over to an empty bench and checked the time on her phone.

Cars sped past, honking and swerving. She'd never been in this part of San Francisco before. Marin checked the map riveted to the wall. Buses moved through the streets all day long, spreading from the transit center like baby centipedes crawling all over the city, and inland to the low hills, and out to the coast.

Number 4 was scheduled to arrive in six minutes. Marin checked the time again. She watched other buses come and go. She watched the people come and go. She tried not to make eye contact with the man sitting on the ground, whose gray beard was matted at the ends and whose mouth never stopped moving.

Marin squirmed on the hard bench. She wished Lucy were here with her.

47

Owls possess exceptional eyesight. They can detect the scurrying of field mice from high in the air. They can pick out details in the dark that you or I couldn't see even with the help of a pair of high-tech night-vision goggles. So it was little trouble at all for Owl to spot the tip of Marin's cardigan draped over the seat behind her as the bus pulled into traffic.

The bones that supported his wings were sore already from his flight across the city. He didn't know how much longer they would hold him aloft. He didn't know how far the little girl would be traveling that day.

OOOOoooo, Owl called as the bus swung west. *OOOOoooo.* He stepped off the roof, spread his wings to catch the air, and glided after her.

48

When the bus dropped Marin at the Manzanita Park and Ride and pulled onto the Shoreline Highway, she waited until it disappeared around a bend in the road. Her ears rang with the absence of noise—the hiss of the brakes, the mumbling of the woman in the seat behind her, and the steady whoosh of cars passing on the highway.

She pulled her phone out of her pocket and opened the map on her screen. A blinking blue dot indicated the spot where she stood. Now that she was standing at the intersection of one highway and another, the coastline where she was headed suddenly seemed very far away.

Marin adjusted her backpack, crossed the road

49

Owl flew over the girl as she walked. A creek was to her right, the briny tang of the marsh behind her, and far beyond, the restless sea. The aluminum bottles in her backpack clanked against each other, and the water inside sloshed with each step. Now that she was moving at the pace of her own legs, Owl could alight on stout branches high above her head and let the sore wing hang limp, the blood pulsing beneath his skin and flaring hot around the mended bones.

The trees along the highway had stood straight and unhindered, reaching for the sky. But the closer Owl flew to the ocean, the squattier the trees got, stung by the salt and blown back by coastal winds day after day.

Once she turned off the highway, there was no

when the light turned, and stepped onto the sidewalk. The blinking dot crept forward. There should be a creek ahead, and just before that, her turn.

From an inn across the street, the smell of burnt coffee rose into the air, and Marin's stomach gave a little gurgle for attention. She had already eaten her string cheese and apple on the bus. She couldn't eat her sandwich yet—she had a long ways still to travel. Perhaps she should have packed a bigger lunch.

more sidewalk, so the girl tramped through the tall grasses beside the winding road. She looked so small down there. Smaller, even, than in the busy city where skyscrapers and cable cars and grown-ups towered over her. What could cause the hatchling to wander so far from home?

It must be something terribly important. It must be something much bigger than herself.

OOOOoooo, Owl thought. *OOOOoooo. The bird who moves a mountain begins by carrying away small stones.*

50

After her first surgery, when Dr. Lucy stripped away the paper gown and mask and gloves and washed the dusting of powder from her hands, she reached for her cell phone. She always messaged the sitter on her way into surgery, so that when she was done, an answer would be waiting for her.

Most times, the answer was a rundown of the day so far: walks to the park or quiet mornings spent reading, and a curious amount of time at a flower shop. But this time there wasn't a message. There were five missed calls and two voice mails.

Lucy lifted the phone to her ear. Her hand trembled.

"Dr. Lucy, it's Alice. I got your message this

morning, but I didn't come in today. I got a text from you last night canceling. I figured you and Marin were going to spend the day together? You're not answering your phone. I don't know what to do. Is she home all alone? I guess you could be in surgery for hours. I'll just go over there, okay? I'll go check on her."

Bewildered, Lucy scrolled through her messages. Sure enough, last night her phone had sent a message canceling for the day. But Lucy certainly hadn't sent that message.

The hand holding the phone dropped to her side as the pieces slid together. *Marin. What have you done?*

Lucy's feet moved her through the doors and to the nurses' station. Her fingers scrolled to the next voice mail.

"Dr. Lucy? I'm at your house and you're not here and there's a note from Marin. Should I read it? I should. I think? Sorry. Okay. It says: 'I had to go find something out. Don't worry.' Dr. Lucy? I'm worried. I'll stay here in case she comes back. I'll call you the minute I hear from her."

There were no more messages.

"Dr. Chang, are you all right?" the nurse asked.

"Cancel the rest of my day."

"But you have two more—"

"Cancel them."

They say that after a new mother births her child and holds it for the very first time, all memory of the agony of childbirth falls away, and the woman discovers an entirely new understanding of love. They say that the new mother's whole being is consumed by the child in her arms. She would give her life to protect it. She would wrestle a charging bear to keep it safe.

When mothering comes in ways other than through the womb, that same moment of transformation still arrives. It shows up at different times, and in other forms, but it comes nonetheless. A woman stops viewing the world as a solitary being, and she becomes a mother.

Lucy felt the shift like a tremor beneath her skin. She ran for the doors. She ran after her daughter.

51

For centuries, the North American Plate and the Pacific Plate have grated against each other. Year by year, day by day, vying for the right to rest in the ground undisturbed, for the privilege of holding up a continent, of balancing oceans and forests and cities above.

But two things cannot occupy the same space. Not mothers. Not wishes. And not tectonic plates. Something has to give.

52

The trailhead was quiet. Nobody else was out there on a Monday morning.

Marin looked around the empty parking lot. She looked at the trailhead and down the gravel path that disappeared over a hill. The little squiggly line on the map that marked the trail from the highway to the trailhead had looked as easy as a brisk walk around the block. She was thirsty, and tired, and the battery on her phone was down to one red sliver. She wanted to stop, to sit on one of the benches beside the trail and not take another step.

She shouldn't even be here. She should be playing in the park or at the museum or reading a book in her room like any other kid. She shouldn't have to chase after her own mother and make her act like one. It wasn't supposed to work like that.

Dr. Lucy wanted her—and not just if she was quiet, and convenient, but however she came and whatever she acted like. Why couldn't her own mother want her half that much?

Marin kept walking. Thin clouds moved across the sun, turning the sky and the ocean on the horizon a brooding gray. When at last the trail opened on a dark sand beach, Marin stumbled over to a wave-washed log and sat. Blisters had formed on her heels and her shoulders ached from where the straps of her backpack had rubbed her skin raw.

Marin's stomach gurgled and she dug the sandwich out of her bag. So what if she didn't have enough for later? She was hungry and she was tired and she was all alone. She was going to eat her lunch. Marin bit into the sandwich, cupping a hand beneath to catch the crumbs.

The waves rolled into the half-moon cove and were sucked back out again. The cliffs on either side cushioned the sound of the surf and the wind and a pair of noisy gulls squabbling over a half-buried morsel.

As she ate, Marin kept glancing out of the corner of her eye to the cliff above. No one was up there, not that she could see. Not yet.

She didn't want to put that backpack on her shoulders ever again. She didn't want to climb up to those cliffs. But she'd come this far. She had to keep going.

So she plodded through the sand, and the grains worked into the weave of her socks and ground like sandpaper against her blisters. Marin started up the side of the cliff. She slipped on the loose pebbles beneath her feet, and before she was halfway up, her palms were scraped and red and her elbow was bleeding. Her hair escaped from its ponytail and stuck to the sweaty skin at her neck and forehead.

When she reached the top, the wind blew across her cheeks, as if in apology. Marin was exhausted. She was scraped and scratched and filthy. She was here— but she wasn't excited, like she thought she would be. She wasn't even nervous. She felt . . . empty. All those times, over all those years, when she had pictured reuniting with her mother, she'd never imagined it would feel like this.

53

Gilda hung up the phone, chucked her heels under her desk, and laced her tennis shoes. She ran down the stairs and into the hired car with its door wide open and waiting for her. Gilda hadn't even finished closing her door when Lucy directed the driver: "Take us to Tennessee Cove, please."

"You sure, lady? It'll take more than an hour, and I'll have to charge you extra for—"

"I don't care what it costs!"

When the car jumped into traffic, Lucy sat back and turned to face the social worker.

"Thank you for coming. I didn't know what else to do." The phone in Lucy's lap displayed a map of the coast with a blinking dot right at the edge of the sand and the water.

"She's run away?"

"I don't know. Maybe."

"You're tracking her cell phone?"

Lucy nodded. The blinking dot stayed in the same spot. "Why would Marin do this? What did I do wrong?"

Gilda shook her head as the car lurched into traffic. "It may have absolutely nothing to do with you. Remember, what Marin has been through is a kind of trauma. Neglect and abandonment may not cause bruising on the outside, but the wounds they leave on the inside sometimes are even more damaging."

"Whatever she needed to do, whatever she went out there for—I would have gone with her. I would have helped her if she would have just asked."

Gilda shifted her weight on the slick vinyl seat. "You know I have to report this, don't you? I'm very sorry to say they probably won't give her back to you after this."

Lucy laid her hand on the social worker's arm, then quickly drew it back again. "No—please don't let them take Marin away from me."

"I'm afraid those are the regulations. Child Protective Services requires that all runaway situations be treated with the standard protocol. This will delay, if not halt altogether, your petition for adoption."

Lucy dropped her head into her hands. "I shouldn't have called you. I just wanted her to be safe. I thought between the pair of us, she would let one of us help her."

Lucy laid her cheek against the cool window and watched the buildings blur as the car sped out of the city.

54

Fog is a funny thing. When you take an out-of-town guest to see the red-cabled bridge over the bay, or out whale watching, or to the pier for a view of Alcatraz, the fog will almost certainly be thick that day, and your efforts will only be spoiled. Similarly, if you're waiting for someone on top of a sea cliff, and you aren't sure if they will walk up this one, or that one on the other side of the cove, the fog will likely roll in so you can't see beyond your fingertips.

It's not that the fog is malicious. It's just highly curious. Being made of such thin stuff, it only wants to be a part of the goings-on of more substantial creatures.

So while Marin waited, the fog pressed in all around her. It laid round droplets of mist on her hair and on the fibers of her cardigan. She pulled her knees up to her chest and stared, not toward the ocean as most visitors to that cliff had done, but inland.

The noon sun passed overhead and took most of the afternoon with it. Marin's food was gone, and one of her water bottles was empty. She hadn't thought to bring a book or a deck of cards to entertain herself while she waited. She'd thought only as far as getting there. It hadn't occurred to her that she might make it to the right cliff at the right time, and nothing would happen.

She dipped her hand into her pocket and felt the three pennies there. She could ask. She could throw the pennies down on the dusty rock and ask the *I Ching* what to do.

But no matter how many times she pulled the pennies from her pocket and stared at their green and copper weight in her open hand, she never did. After all those years of casting and asking and wishing for a way back to her mother, now that Marin was there, nothing was as she thought it would be. She knew her mother's name, and her birthday, and her favorite place in the world. She could call to mind the memory of her face eclipsing the sun, and the dark curls brushing against Marin's skin.

She knew that memory. She knew the story by

heart that she had created to go with it—who her mother was and how perfect everything would be when they found each other again. But Marin didn't know Summer Greene, not really. And now that Marin was there, on the foggy cliff, waiting for Summer to climb up the path at any moment, she was suddenly unsure about everything she had thought she knew.

55

Marin hadn't meant to fall asleep. But when a puff of grit from the hardscrabble cliffs rolled over her face and her eyes were startled open, she found herself looking at a horizontal world. There, on the ground in front of her, were a pair of Birkenstocked feet. Marin tilted her head and looked up. She couldn't see the person's face—it was no more than a shadow blocking out the sun and dark, curling locks swinging toward the ground.

Marin brushed the grit from her cheeks and wrapped wayward strands of her hair behind her ears. "Mother?"

The wind snatched the word out of her mouth and swirled it around the woman who stood over her, the belled sleeves of her batik blouse whipping and the white fringe of her ripped jeans flapping in the air.

Marin sat up and tried again, squinting into the shadowed face. "You're Summer Greene."

"I am."

Marin stood and dusted off her clothes. "Then you're my mother."

The woman turned and looked out at the water. Her nose was sharper than Marin remembered, and there were creases at the corners of her eyes and mouth that hadn't been there before.

But it was her.

"I haven't been called that in a very long time." Summer turned and regarded the girl in front of her, and Marin noticed, for the first time, that she held something in her hands. It was a ceramic frog with a slot carved into the head for coins. "And it's not who I am. I knew almost from the start that mothering wasn't my path."

Marin pulled the waistband of her cardigan down to her hips. She hugged her arms over her stomach.

Summer ticked her head to the side. "You do look like me, though—the eyes for sure, and that's your grandfather's chin." She set the frog down on the ground. "I suppose you have questions. That seems fair. Okay, ask."

Nothing was going how Marin had planned. There was no running to meet each other, no desperate embrace, no heartfelt apologies. If anything, it seemed like Summer was irritated that Marin was there at all.

Marin didn't have any questions prepared. She hadn't known she was going to need them. It had never occurred to her that this beginning might also be an end, that if she ever wanted to know anything about the woman who had brought her into the world, she had to ask it now.

Marin took a step toward Summer, away from the cliff's edge and into the wind. "Why didn't you leave information on how I could reach you? If you had to go away for a while, why didn't you drop me off with an aunt or grandma or somebody who might try to care for me? Why did you just leave me to be passed around by strangers?" Marin's voice wobbled as if someone had taken her by the shoulders and shook her until the questions tumbled out.

"Why didn't you ever come back?"

"There was nobody to leave you with. It was just you and me." Summer flipped her long curls over her shoulder and took a deep breath. "Anyway, I'm not your mother, not really. I'm just the person who birthed you. Mothers are selfless and patient and steady. I am none of those things. And it was pretty obvious I was never going to be. Wouldn't you rather have a chance for a new mother than be stuck with somebody who doesn't want the job?"

"Of course I—"

"Don't answer that. How did you find me, anyway? Why did you even go looking for me?"

Marin drew in a shaky breath. This was her chance, maybe her only chance. "I want us to be a family again."

Summer just stared at her, uncomprehending. She lifted her arms and let them drop, slapping her sides as they fell. Finally, she sputtered, "What kind of kid wants a mother who doesn't want her back?"

It may have been just a tree falling in the inland forest, or a section of cliffside plunging into the waves below, but to Marin, the *crack* that rippled over the cliff she stood on and echoed through the cove may as well have been the whole world breaking apart.

Her mother didn't want her. Not now. Not ever.

That's what the kids at her last foster home had said, and Talula, and even Gilda Blackbourne. Marin hadn't believed them. But all along, all this time, they had been right.

Her legs suddenly remembered the long morning spent walking, and she sank to the ground. The wind swirled through the cove and blasted up the hillside, snatching the first hot tears from her eyelashes.

"Marin!" The voice was faint over the ringing in the girl's ears, and the crashing of the surf, and the breaking of the world. But the shouts didn't stop, and they came steadily closer. *"Marin!"*

There, down on the beach below, was Lucy, still in the mint-green scrubs she'd worn into surgery. Sweat stains ringed her armpits, and her hair, which was normally smooth as silk and neat about her face, whipped in the wind, strands clinging to her eyes and the corners of her mouth.

Gilda, several steps behind her, dropped her hands to her knees and exhaled in deep, heaving breaths. Clearly the social worker was not accustomed to tearing through underbrush and hiking through deep sand in the regular execution of her work.

Lucy ran around the cove, through the thick sand that dragged her back with each step. By the time she reached the base of the cliff, Marin was already hurtling down to meet her. The girl skidded on the loose bits of rock and wheeled her arms to keep her balance, but she didn't stop running. When at last she reached the sand, Marin hid her face in the doctor's shoulder and wound her arms tight around her foster mother's neck.

Lucy may have cast a withering look to the cliff and the solitary woman who gripped the clay creature in her hands and smashed it against the rock, then began offering bits of paper to the greedy wind.

But Marin didn't look back once.

56

Owl watched the girl and her guardians slowly cross the dark sands and make their way to the trailhead that would lead them home. She was safe; Owl could go home now. His head swiveled to the lone figure on the cliff and the wind that snatched and pulled at her clothes.

Owl clicked his beak and tasted the brine on the air, and the moon rising against a pale sky, and the lingering hurt in the saltwater tears that had rolled down the little girl's face.

OOOOoooo, he thought. *OOOOoooo*.

He would have to begin the long flight home soon. The winds would fight him the whole time if he kept to the coastline, though the way would be much shorter. Owl leaped off the branch of the wind-sheared evergreen where he'd rested. He let his wings drift him low to the ground in a gentle glide. Every few hundred yards he alighted on a tree or the cupola of a lighthouse, or the trusses of the red-cabled bridge across the bay.

OOOOoooo, Owl thought. *OOOOoooo. It matters not how slowly you go, so long as you do not stop.*

57

The drive over the Golden Gate Bridge and back into the city was quiet, though three people now occupied the backseat. Gilda kept to her side and stared straight forward. It was her obligation to be there, to go where she had been called. But she couldn't shake the feeling that her presence was an intrusion in some private space.

Beside her, Marin lay across the center seat, her head resting on her foster mother's lap and her wind-ruffled hair hiding her face from view. Dr. Lucy sat perfectly still so she wouldn't disturb Marin, though her arms lay protectively over the girl's shoulders and cradled her head.

A small feeling of unease swirled inside Gilda and

settled like a stone in the pit of her stomach. She had to report this. It was her duty. If she didn't follow protocol, then what point was there to anything she did all day long?

But perhaps Marin hadn't really meant to run away. She had left a note, after all. And the way Lucy watched over the girl in her lap . . .

No. There were rules. Rules existed to be followed.

Gilda had no choice. She would file the report first thing in the morning.

58

Some days are so awful, you can't imagine things will ever get better, and you definitely would never believe they could get even worse. Marin lay on her twin bed so still that hardly a wrinkle mussed the sheets. The pillow was tucked under the bedspread, and Marin smooshed her face into the crease. Her pennies were scattered across the room where she had hurled them out of her pocket, and the *I Ching* lay open, facedown, a thin crack running the length of the spine where she had stamped her heel into it.

Lucy had poked her head into Marin's room a few times since they'd gotten back from the beach, once with a plate of food, once with a mug of hot chocolate brimming with melting marshmallows, and once just to check that she was still there. Lucy didn't need to say she was worried and confused and sad. All that was plain as could be, and it only made Marin hide her face even deeper in the covers.

Most of us can rely on something good in our lives. Our parents' love. The constancy of a family pet. A pesky little sister or a know-it-all older brother and the perpetual flip-flop of siblings between affection and annoyance. For as long as she could remember, Marin had only two things she could rely on: the idea that her mother was out there, just like her, waiting to be reunited, and that the *I Ching* would lead Marin to her.

Everything she'd believed was a lie. There was nothing good she could count on.

The little bed rocked beneath her. The empty hangers in the closet clattered together like cascading dominoes. The window blinds buckled and slapped against the glass.

Sympathetic creatures, to care so much about the little girl who shared the room with them. Or so she thought. But suddenly everything was noise—blaring car alarms from the street below and the shrill groan of bending steel. Marin shot upright. And then everything was moving, shaking, pitching wildly in all directions at once. Marin opened her mouth to scream, but nothing came out.

"Marin!" Lucy flung the door open. "Quick—get over here beneath the desk."

Marin stumble-fell to the floor and crawled across the buckling carpet. The floor shook again, knocking her flat. This time she did scream, and Lucy was there, her hands beneath Marin's armpits, dragging her across the carpet. The two of them crammed into the space beneath the desk, their arms wrapped around each other and their legs bent at awkward angles beneath them.

The walls trembled and the window exploded, showering cubes of glass like water sparkling from a fountain. Outside the sky was full of birds—gulls and squawking crows and even an owl with a hitch in his wing strokes—flying as far away from the quaking earth as they could get.

Below the window, the dresser tipped forward on two legs. The drawers banged open and the piggy bank scooted inch by inch to the dresser's edge.

"No!" Marin cried. She jerked forward, but Lucy's arms held her tight. The piggy bank crashed to the floor and shattered into jagged shards that quivered and leaped across the carpet.

"*Shhhh,*" Lucy said, and she rocked back and forth, holding Marin as if she were a much younger girl. "I'm here. *Shhhh.*"

The ground rumbled and the bridges swayed. Trees that had stood straight and tall since the previous century shook the dirt from their roots and tumbled to the earth.

In every home across the city, keepsakes shattered and walls cracked, pipes burst and paintings crashed to the floor. While everything around them shook at the mercy of the shuddering tectonic plates, people clung to one another. They held tight to what mattered.

59

The view of the city from above may as well have been of a different world. The fog, like a tufted blanket, muffled the sound of cracking sidewalks and steaming pipes.

Owl circled above San Francisco, his wings stretched as wide as they could go to loft him high above the breaking city. His wing with the knitted-together bones throbbed. But it wasn't safe to land, not yet.

The air all around him was full. Ravens flapped haphazardly, cawing their distress. Songbirds fluttered and flitted, struggling to rise higher than they knew they should.

OOOOoooo, Owl keened. *OOOOoooo. Our greatest glory is not in never falling but in rising every time we fall.*

60

Even something as terrifying as an earthquake can't last forever. Eventually, the shaking stopped. The sound of car alarms dimmed one by one, and blaring sirens took their place.

Lucy crawled out from under the desk. She reached a hand to help Marin up, and they collapsed back together for a long moment, each holding tight to the other.

"We should get out of the building," Lucy said into Marin's hair, "in case a gas line burst."

Marin nodded.

Lucy darted through the house. She grabbed food and water bottles, a jacket for each of them, and sturdy walking shoes. She ducked into Marin's room and emerged a few minutes later, tugging the zipper to Marin's backpack closed.

Lucy pocketed her cell phone, shouldered the backpack, and they walked together to the stairwell, down eleven flights of stairs, and outside.

The fog was gone. The sun shone bright against a blue sky. They stood there a moment, blinking at the sky, empty of birds, empty of fog, empty of airplanes, empty.

Lucy's phone buzzed in her pocket. Without even looking at it, she squeezed Marin's hand and said, "They'll need me at the hospital. Some people won't have been as lucky as us, and they'll be hurt." Her eyes pooled, and slow tears traveled down her cheeks and splashed against the broken sidewalk. "But I don't want to leave you alone right now. Will you come with me to the hospital?"

Marin nodded again, and this time she looked up. She saw the tears rolling down her foster mother's cheeks and dripping off her chin. Marin remembered the empty chambers in Lucy's heart, and the one that was already full. She squeezed Lucy's hand back. "I don't want to leave you alone right now either."

They walked, hand in hand, dodging cracks in the sidewalk. The streets were empty except for a few dogs running back and forth, barking, and a yowling cat whose tail stuck straight up in the air like a chimney brush. In the distance, sirens wailed and fire trucks blasted their horns. Lucy and Marin picked their way carefully through the rubble. When they rounded the last corner, the hospital was lit up, its doors wide open and beckoning.

A nurse ran to meet them. "Dr. Chang! Thank goodness you're here. They need you on the third floor." So they ran, all together, into the hospital and up the stairs.

There was a waiting room on the third floor, within view of the nurses' station. Lucy sat on a couch in the corner and Marin settled beside her.

"I have to go into surgery now," Lucy said as she unzipped the backpack and pulled out Marin's things one by one. "That woman behind the desk is named Viola. If you need anything at all, you ask her, okay?"

Marin eyed the woman in the daisy-covered scrubs. Viola waved and flashed a preoccupied smile in the girl's direction.

"I'll be a few hours, so here are some snacks, some books, and a blanket if you get cold. I need you to stay right here so I know you're safe. Can you do that?"

"Sure."

"I mean it," Dr. Lucy said, gripping Marin's hand. "There are people in there who really need me right now and I can't do my job if I'm worried about you."

"I'll be right here."

"Okay," Lucy said. She squeezed Marin's hand one last time and stood.

"Wait—what's this?" Marin asked, poking a knotted plastic bag.

"Oh." Lucy pulled the knots free so Marin could look inside. "It's your piggy bank that broke. I threw some superglue in the bag. You can try to put it back together if that's what you want. Or I can help you later, or we can go pick out another one. I'm sorry, Marin, I know it was important to you."

Marin peeked inside the bag. There were the ceramic shards, the undersides bone white. And the nickel. And a bunch of scraps of paper. Marin lifted one. "What are these?"

"I don't know—they were inside the piggy bank. Marin, I have to go now. Are you going to be all right here?"

Marin felt her head bobbing up and down, nodding. She felt Lucy kiss the top of her head and heard her jog across to the swinging doors. But all that was dim background noise. After all this time, she finally understood. She held the folded scraps of paper in her hands.

They were wishes.

61

*I wish I could start running and not stop until I reach
the tip of South America.*

*I wish I could float up to the clouds and never come
down.*

I wish I knew how to be a mother.

I wish I was free.

Summer's handwriting was slanted, a scrawling cursive that didn't care so much for things like crossed *T*s or dotted *I*s. But the feeling in those words pulsed through the scraps of paper and into the pads of Marin's fingers.

These were her mother's words. Her wishes. At least the ones she got down in the months before she'd left seven years ago. Marin's hands shook as she unbent the crinkled papers one fold at a time.

I wish I could climb to the top of a cypress tree and live there, drinking the clouds and eating nothing but the wet, clean air.

I wish I could make my daughter happy.

I wish I knew what to do.

Marin had always thought of her mother as someone who just got confused about what she wanted and where she was supposed to be. But those weren't the wishes of a woman who doesn't know what she wants. Those were the wishes of a woman who knows what she wants, only she can't ever have it, not unless she does a terrible thing.

I wish I could swim to the center of the ocean buoyed up by a school of manta rays vaulting in the waves all around me.

I wish I could leave everything behind.

I wish better for Marin than me.

Some things are too much for an eleven-year-old girl to understand. For instance, what makes some women mothers and others not. Or why adults do things they'll only regret for the rest of their lives. But that last wish—that she understood.

I wish better for Marin than me.

Marin stood and one by one dropped the shards of her broken piggy bank into the trash. And the wishes too. All except the last one. The last wish she pressed between the pages of her pocket-size *I Ching*, which Lucy had tucked into the front of her backpack. That one she wanted to remember.

She might never understand her mother. But they agreed on one thing.

Marin wanted better for herself too.

62

When the dust settled and the buildings ceased their creaking, Owl's wide circles above the city drifted lower and lower. His right wing ached where the bone had broken so many years ago. *OOOOoooo*, he burbled each time he flapped to steady himself after a wild burst of wind.

The city block where he had lived since the old man, his teacher, had died still looked more or less the same. The new buildings were unscathed, only missing some windows here and there. But the older structures leaned precariously, and a few roofs had fallen in. It wasn't until he was nearly on top of it that he realized that the stovepipe where he'd roosted was crushed. He couldn't fit inside anymore.

Owl landed on the roof and looked across the canyon between buildings to the little girl's room. The window was shattered. It was dark inside. No one moved within.

OOOOoooo, Owl thought. *OOOOoooo*. It wasn't safe out in the open during the day. If he was going to make it to the forest, he should leave now. His wings were tired after keeping aloft for so long during the earthquake, and he would have to stop and rest several times on the way.

He opened his wings to fly, only to close them. Who would watch over the hatchling if he left? He leaped off the roof, gliding over the street below. He settled on the windowsill of the little girl's bedroom. The room was empty.

Owls are private creatures. They prefer to venture out in the darkness, when waking eyes are closed for the night. Owl flexed his talons, one foot, then the other, his claws slipping on the polished stone. To remain on the windowsill, in full view of the passersby below, would be ill-advised. It wasn't safe. He should go. Owl opened his wings, then he closed them again. He couldn't leave, not without knowing if the little girl was all right.

OOOOoooo, Owl thought. *OOOOoooo*. *Act with kindness, but do not expect gratitude.*

63

When friction builds and builds and builds and finally releases, a long, languorous breath moves through the earth. Instead of grinding and gnashing against each other, the Pacific Plate and the North American Plate learned to brush companionably beside each other for a while. Before long the friction would rise, until one day it would ripple up and out over the city again.

But for now, and for a while to come, the earth was at peace with itself, and all those who lived above could settle comfortably in.

64

Lucy felt like her insides had been scraped bare. Every earthquake did that to her. She tried, on most days, not to focus on what she had lost. But on days when the earth shook, it was impossible to keep her grief at bay. The surgeries had been lengthy, but necessary, the weight of the loved ones waiting for word holding her in the operating room well after midnight.

It had been a long night, and a slow walk home. Lucy didn't even have the energy to check if the oven worked, much less to boil water for a cup of tea. Her building had been declared safe, and that was all that mattered. She sat at the edge of her bed, where Marin would sleep that night, and smoothed the covers over the girl's shoulders.

"You didn't fix your piggy bank?"

"It wasn't mine. It was my mo—. It belonged to Summer."

Lucy nodded. "Do you want to talk about it?"

"No," Marin said. "But I do want to talk to Gilda Blackbourne. Can we call her tomorrow?"

Lucy blinked at the ceiling. She turned her head toward the open doorway and blinked some more. "Sure."

She patted Marin's arm and left the room. The thing about an organ as fragile as a heart is that it can stand only so many surgical interventions before it fails entirely. Lucy closed the door behind her and let the tears roll down her cheeks in the dark hallway.

She cried for herself, because she was too tired not to. She cried for the woman she had loved so bravely, so brashly. And she cried for the girl on the other side of the door, whom she had almost let herself believe would be her daughter.

65

The following day, when the elevator doors closed in front of Gilda Blackbourne with a *whoosh* that sent her hair reeling backward, and she was carried soundlessly back to the ground, the polished brass reflected what can only be called a conflicted face.

Her report on the runaway had been written, and it would have been filed that morning if the earthquake hadn't shut down business for the better part of the day. It *would* be filed, just as soon as her office reopened.

Gilda was objective. She followed procedures. She made no exceptions. She had been absolutely determined not to be wooed. But as the elevator dinged, the doors glided open, and the white-gloved doorman ushered her out onto the street, even Gilda herself was not convinced.

66

For half a day, instead of a window, there was an open portal to the sky in Marin's bedroom. After the earthquake, Lucy had cleared away all the little bricks of broken glass and promptly called the glass company.

Now there was a brand-new window, even if it was only temporary. This one was a slider missing its screen—it was the best the glass company could do with all the calls they had taken that day. Lucy made Marin promise to keep the window shut, but the girl soon discovered that if she left it open while she slept at night, the fog drifted in and left pinprick drops of moisture on her cheeks. Sure, the garbage trucks made an awful racket in the morning, but then that meant she was awake to watch the sunrise reflected in the windows across the street.

It wasn't until the third night after the earthquake that she noticed the windowsill wasn't precisely unoccupied. Perhaps it was the sound of ruffling feathers, or the delicate clicking of sharp talons on stone, that woke her in the middle of the night. The moon was bright, so even though she couldn't see well through her sleep-blurred eyes, she could certainly tell that the bright rectangle held a large, dark shadow in its center.

Marin blinked and a pair of round eyes blinked back at her.

"Hello?" she asked.

OOOOoooo, Owl replied.

The girl sat up and rubbed her eyes. Yes, there was a large bird perched in her open window. Marin eyed the talons that gripped the window ledge. The bird opened his wings and shook the feathers out; one wing opened slightly lower than the other.

"Oh, you can't fly so well, can you?" Marin whispered, so Lucy wouldn't hear and wake in the other room. Her fear fell away like the bits of down swishswaying to the street below. She peeled back her covers. "Would you like to come in? No? Would you like something to eat? We don't have any mice or ground squirrels or the other sorts of things an owl might like."

Owl shifted his weight from one foot to the other. "Or I could read to you?"

OOOOoooo, Owl replied.

And so the girl pulled her pocket-size *I Ching* out of her desk drawer and sat in the wooden chair, pulling her knees to her chest and propping the little book there. She had read the book cover to cover so many times that she could speak the words while only giving them half her attention. The other half wondered what those downy feathers might feel like, what those huge wings would look like in midflight, and what on earth that owl was doing at her window. She read, and she watched him, and she wondered, if she built him a home out there, maybe out of the apple crate in the pantry, if he would stay.

The following morning, Marin slept straight through the sunrise and the banging, braking trash trucks. When she finally did wake, the window was an empty rectangle again. Perhaps she had dreamed the whole thing. But no—on the farthest edge of the sill was a single feather, curving upward at the tips like a grin.

67

Government agencies are not known for the speed of their decision making. For those awaiting news from one of those entities, days can feel like weeks, and the hours within can seem to stretch on forever.

Lucy and Marin stood together before the tall windows overlooking the city. Lucy sipped a cup of chamomile tea to try to soothe her nerves while Marin stirred chocolate syrup into a tall glass of milk.

"Do you want to tell me about your talk with Gilda?" Lucy asked.

Marin paused her stirring and looked up at her foster mother. "I explained to Ms. Blackbourne that you and I are like two halves of a bone trying to connect after a bad break. Now that we've started growing together, we'll be stronger than before."

Lucy swallowed several times, but she did not speak.

"Is that right? Did I get the medical part right?" Marin whispered.

Lucy nodded. And she answered, even though her voice wavered and broke, "You've got it exactly right, Marin."

68

"When are the repair people coming back again to fix my window?" Marin asked in between bites of sugary wheat squares.

"Oh, not until next week, I think. They're really backed up with all the broken windows in the city. Is the slider in your bedroom bothering you?" Lucy frowned the way she did when she was wondering if she had, yet again, made some terrible parenting misstep. Was the missing screen a hazard? Would Child Protective Services take Marin away from her if they knew? "Maybe we should nail some boards across the window for now."

"No!" Marin chewed and swallowed. "I like it."

Lucy raised her mug of tea to her lips and blew across the top.

"In fact, I was wondering if, instead of just a glass

pane, can I keep the sliding one, so I can open it sometimes?"

Lucy took a sip of her tea. Marin's cheeks were just the slightest bit pink, and Lucy had been watching her charge carefully enough to know this meant something, even if she wasn't entirely sure what that something was. "I'll think about it."

A knock sounded at the door. Lucy placed a lid on her mug, slung her briefcase over her shoulder, and hurried to let Alice in. "I'm going to the hospital now, but I have the day off tomorrow. Should we take a trip to the beach?"

Marin nodded vigorously, and she jumped down off her stool to hug her foster mother before she left. While Lucy traveled down to the ground floor, Marin ran to the window. Most days, when Lucy's head became visible below, it was only a quick few steps before she reached the corner.

But that day, she paused and knelt to observe something on the sidewalk directly below the window to Marin's room. It was a little ball of fur and bones. A pellet. Lucy peered up at the bedroom window and her eyes narrowed as she noticed the apple crate perched there.

When she reached the corner and waved, Marin waved back, though her cheeks were full red and burning by then.

69

A cross town, in a courtroom filled only with empty jurors' chairs and empty audience seats, Gilda Blackbourne opened a wind-battered case file. One by one, she handed documents to the judge. One to demonstrate that Marin had no blood relatives who wished to keep her. One to demonstrate that Lucy Chang was able, fit, and most eager to adopt the girl.

Gilda closed the file and clasped her hands in front of her. No single thing in her professional career came close to the gratification she felt while hurtling over that final strip of red tape in front of her.

The judge fixed her with a calculating stare. "And you know of no reason why this child should not be placed with this woman? There have been no irregularities? No breaches of protocol in the course of the guardianship?"

"None, Your Honor. An open-and-shut case if I've ever seen one."

On a different day, the judge might have ordered an extension of the trial period. If Gilda Blackbourne had one iota less of a reputation for being a woman who relished strict adherence to rules and regulations, he may have decided differently. But he didn't.

The judge tapped his gavel against the block. His pen scrawled across the signature line.

And just like that, Lucy and Marin belonged to each other.

ilda delivered the news herself. She kicked off her heels, wiggled her toes in the plush carpet, and popped the cork on a fizzing bottle of cider. Rules be hanged, she swept Marin and Lucy in a crushing hug.

Lucy brought out crystal goblets and Gilda poured golden bubbles into each until they overflowed. All three rushed to drink, laughing as their mouths filled with effervescence.

The paint on the high-ceilinged walls hadn't been changed. The furniture had not been arranged any differently than the last time Gilda visited. The newly installed panes of safety glass were no less intimidating. But the apartment felt different, all the same. Softer, perhaps. Or warmer. Definitely not empty. Not at all.

When the bubbles in her goblet had subsided, Marin tilted her head toward Lucy. "I've been thinking."

"Yes?" Lucy replied.

"Instead of a cat, can we have an owl?"

71

Out on the windowsill, Owl opened his eyes to greet the deepening dark. It was a foggy night, bad for hunting, good for fluffing up one's feathers and watching the blinking city lights diffused and dispersed by the droplets of water on the air.

He thought about his teacher, who, when he had grown old and frail, tried again and again to release Owl into the woods, where birds of prey were supposed to live. But every time, Owl had returned to his teacher's side. He had stayed with the old man to the very end, so that his teacher, who had cared for him all those years, would have someone to see him through his final days.

Owl thought about his girl inside and the mother

she had chosen. He could have launched off the windowsill, knowing she was safe, knowing she had landed in her nest. But he had some choosing of his own to do. Owl shook the mist from his feathers and tucked his beak beneath them as the plumes settled back over his skin.

OOOOoooo, Owl thought. *OOOOoooo. Wheresoever you go, go with all your heart.*

And he did.

AUTHOR'S NOTE

Approximately 400,000 kids currently live in foster care in the United States. Some children are eventually reunited with their birth families, while some are adopted by new ones. Unfortunately, thousands of youth age out of the foster care system each year and enter adulthood without a family to lean on for support and love.

Every foster kid's experience is unique; Marin's story is just one out of many. And while she is a fictional character, her desires to be seen, valued, and loved are universal ones. Occasionally, in the writing of this book, I accelerated timelines and adjusted specific details of the foster-adopt process for the benefit of the story. I hope those of you who work in and live with the system on a daily basis will forgive these small liberties I've taken.

Over the many months I've spent with Marin, Lucy, and Gilda (and yes, Owl too), these characters have come to occupy a very special place in my heart. So, too, have the real-life foster kids, foster and adoptive parents, and social workers who live a version of this story every day. Thank you for all that you do to make sure these kids can have lives full of hope, opportunity, and all the love they desire.

To learn more, please reach out to your state's foster care support organizations.

Many thanks to . . .

Reka Simonsen

Ammi-Joan Paquette

Justin Chanda

Lauren Rille

Tom Daly

Victo Ngai

Jeannie Ng

Kristin Derwich

Michelle Karcher